Ready
Or
Not

Doreen M. Bleich

PublishAmerica
Baltimore

First printing

ISBN: 1-59129-440-1
PUBLISHED BY
PUBLISHAMERICA BOOK PUBLISHERS
www.publishamerica.com
Baltimore

Printed in the United States of America

Dedicated to Lois W. – without the confidence and encouragement of the program and friends in the fellowship, I would not have even dared to dream this dream.

Acknowledgements

I wish to express my appreciation to the following:
Dorothy Wark for her work on the cover design and
photos; Helen Perrin Clarke for her many hours of
proofreading and editing work; Dr. Barb Walley for
sharing her medical expertise and all those women
who shared their breast cancer stories.

CHAPTER ONE

The soothing sounds of the organ playing "A Closer Walk With Thee" confirmed what Maggie suspected. She was late. Silently, the heavy oak door closed slowly behind her as she strained her eyes in the dimly lit church foyer to find a spot into which she could slip unnoticed. An usher motioned her forward to an empty seat. Maggie squeezed into the place meant for a midget but was grateful she would not have to stand. The funeral had just begun. The church was full, even the old choir loft.

The deceased, Mr. Anthony John Sanders, was a highly respected man in Nipawin, having taught at the junior high school for more years than Maggie could recall. Sadness had engulfed her when she'd heard the news of Mr. Sanders' death, as it did everyone else in town. He had been her English teacher for two years, but, more importantly, he'd won her respect and that of most of her classmates with his genuine concern and caring. She would miss seeing him out walking his energetic, rambunctious Mitzi, a Jack Russell terrier. She would miss his familiar presence in church, in the fifth row from the back. Nothing stays the same, she thought, no matter how much she wished it would.

Glancing around today, Maggie recognized several of her former teachers and fellow students. Most were teary-eyed. Nipawin, with a population of five thousand souls, was where the Sanders family had lived for over forty years. Most of those attending the funeral today were here out of respect for Mr. Sanders and his family.

Directly across the aisle, looking smug and generally pleased with herself, sat Mathilda Evans. The war between the liberal thinking Mr. Sanders and the ultraconservative Miss Evans was legendary. The entire school population and therefore the community knew of their differences and their battles. She had now outlived him. The final word would be hers.

7

A.J. Sanders' oldest friend, Max Foger, gave a moving eulogy. He spoke of A.J.'s life, community involvements, and his special love for young people. Twice he halted and gazed at the brass urn sitting on the purple-draped table. Vases filled with cheerful yellow tulips surrounded the urn. Reverend Adams did the readings and gave the blessings. A time of fellowship and sharing with the family was scheduled to follow immediately in the church hall downstairs. Everyone was invited. The organ chimed, and the choir, which consisted of many of Mr. Sanders contemporaries, sang "How Great Thou Art" as the family filed out.

Maggie wiped her tears, relieved that the service was over. Going to funerals wasn't her favorite pastime. Since her mother's illness, she prayed nightly that the next funeral she attended wouldn't be someone in her family.

She caught sight of Joan and Wayne Sanders leaving with their children, Max and Jessie. Another couple, who Maggie presumed were Wayne's brother and his family, followed them. Then, a big burly man with sandy-colored hair swept to the side, head down, his arm wrapped protectively about the shoulders of a frail, slightly bowed lady, smartly dressed in purple. This fellow looked like he had come from practice with the Saskatchewan Roughriders and had forgotten to take off the shoulder pads. Who was this guy? Maggie wondered. Could he possibly be Phil Sanders? The party animal, skirt chasing Phil? Couldn't be! The last time Maggie had seen Phil, he was sixteen, over six feet tall, skinny, with a bush of long unruly blondish hair.

Checking her watch as her turn came to leave the church, Maggie decided she would go downstairs for a minute to offer her condolences and say hello to Joan and Wayne, then hurry back to work. Lyle Gaines, her boss at Tobin Lake Motors wasn't happy to have both Maggie and Joan out of the office at the same time. It meant he would have to answer the phone and deal with customers directly, something he loathed. He said that was why he paid her and Joan such good money. That became the office joke.

She spotted Joan off to one side, talking to the lady in purple. She recognized many of the people who were filling up the tables already set for lunch with the church's 50th Anniversary china.

"Hi, Maggie! Thank you for coming. Let me introduce Wayne's Aunt Clara," said Joan as Maggie approached them. "Maggie, this is Clara Morgan. She is A.J.'s youngest sister from Victoria, and now the sole remaining member of her generation of Sanders." Maggie extended her hand. Aunt Clara's grip and twinkling hazel eyes indicated she was not as feeble as her posture suggested. "Aunt Clara, this is Maggie Mills. We work together at Tobin Lake Motors. She's the receptionist."

"I'm pleased to meet you, Mrs. Morgan. Mr. Sanders was a remarkable man, and I for one will miss him."

"We'll all miss Tony. To most people he was A.J., but to me, he was my big brother Tony." She paused, took a breath, and straightened her shoulders in a no-nonsense, get-on-with-life attitude.

"I hope you had a pleasant flight out," Maggie continued.

"The flight was smooth. Ron, my nephew, met the plane in Saskatoon and I came here with them yesterday."

"Will you be staying to sample a bit of March weather in Saskatchewan?"

"I'll stay until Sunday, when Ron and Kathy go back, then fly home Monday morning." Pausing, she added, "I remember vividly what this country can do in March. I was raised here, you know, but I can tell you that I much prefer Victoria's climate. Much better for an old lady's bones," she chuckled.

"What kind of stories are you telling now, Aunt Clara?" asked the unknown man, gently placing his immense hands on her shoulders. Aunt Clara shrunk instantly next to his rugged frame. Maggie's attention shifted to his soft chestnut brown eyes. His right eye twitched slightly.

"Is she going on about winters when they were kids on the prairie? How they walked barefoot two miles to school every day? Uphill both ways!" he teased. The corners of his generous mouth curled up to form dimples low in his cheeks. His gaze met Maggie's.

Joan interrupted with a light touch on his sleeve, "Phil, don't give Aunt Clara a bad time." Nodding toward Maggie, she asked, "You remember Maggie Mills? She was in my class. We work together now."

Phil's attention switched from Maggie's deep magnetic blue eyes to the rest of her.

"Maggie, you must remember my brother-in-law, Phil. You probably won't believe this, but he now teaches at Carlton Comprehensive High School in Prince Albert."

Maggie shot Joan a disbelieving look.

Joan nodded, grinning impishly.

"I'm sorry. I wouldn't have recognized you either," Phil apologized before either could say another word. He extended his hand toward Maggie.

She could feel the heat radiating from his palm to hers and up her arm as he gripped her hand. It was slightly rough, his fingers thick and blunt.

He brazenly scrutinized her from head to toe. She was no waif of a woman. Her large frame was well proportioned, her auburn, collar-length hair was gathered at the nape of her neck with a large gold clip. A variegated red scarf peered from the front of her jacket, hinting at the cleavage just beneath the open top button. The word regal came to his mind.

Suddenly Maggie felt very self-conscious about her size and appearance. This rarely happened anymore. She'd never been the lank and lean type, but there were times when she wished she were – like now. In that instant, the scales tipped in favor of irrational thoughts. She wished she'd skipped lunch. That would make her look thinner. She could have worn her black pumps. They made her taller. Had she remembered to refresh her lipstick before rushing out of the office? Enough already, her brain screamed.

Finding her voice, she replied, "It's been a long time. Seventeen or eighteen years. You have changed." She hoped the warmth she felt spreading throughout her body was not showing. Her hand went round her neck, tugging the scarf higher to cover the red blotches she knew had risen there. Why was she reacting like a silly fool? She'd better make her exit before she embarrassed herself. She reminded herself that what Phil Sanders thought was of no concern to her.

"I delude myself into thinking that this is the mature, scholarly look," Phil replied, running a huge tanned hand down his chest, unbuttoning his jacket somewhat self-consciously.

"Mature is definitely an accurate word to describe both of us," Maggie replied lightly, amused by his antics. She could see he wasn't any more comfortable than she was.

The walk back to the office was much more leisurely than the panic to get to the church. She sighed with relief, breathed deeply of the fresh spring air. Even the weather seemed warmer, more inviting now that the funeral was over.

Lyle fled to his office upon her return. The rest of the afternoon passed in a blur as she worked to get caught up and cover for Joan as well.

Donning her coat and boots, Maggie decided to take the long way home after work. The snow banks, streaked with dirt, were knee-high along Railway Avenue. Patches of black ice were reminders of last week's thaw. Maggie squinted into the brilliant tangerine-hued late afternoon sun over the rim of towering black spruce past River Street.

Traffic scurried along Railway Avenue. The stately grain elevators to her right commanded one side of the street adjacent to the railroad tracks, while on the other were older bungalows with snowmen and sculpted ice animals in the front yards.

The clean air cleared away the cobwebs of the day as she turned off Railway Avenue toward her apartment in Princess Place. Unpolluted, sweet air should be on the list of attractions this town had to offer. It was one of the things she liked best about being back home – the air quality and closeness to the earth. In this part of Saskatchewan, the people were more in tune with nature's changing colors than the latest urban fads. Maggie realized that she was as "at-home" here as anywhere she'd ever lived. Nipawin fit her like a well-worn, cozy pair of flannel pajamas.

Her thoughts drifted to Phil Sanders. He looked more like a football player than a teacher. She tried to imagine him standing in front of twenty-five hormone-driven teenagers spouting the chemical properties of the elements. Or maybe on the football field barking commands, demonstrating tackles, and discussing strategies. The picture of Phil in shorts and a jersey, broad and muscled without the padding, legs like telephone poles, made her shiver. She pulled her collar tighter. But he was still the same flirt he'd been in high school. Remembering his lazy smile and dancing chocolate eyes, the voice in her head reminded her – never trust a man with brown eyes! He couldn't be taken seriously. He was only flirting with her.

Maggie had her life all figured out. It was perfect just as it was. There was no need for a change. Becoming involved with another man was not part of her plan. She had learned her lesson and wasn't about to make the same mistake twice in the same lifetime!

CHAPTER TWO

With her hands firmly curled around her earthenware mug, Maggie watched the shadows cast by the early morning sun streaming through the pine trees. They swayed hypnotically across her table. She had slept badly, dreaming of puny, withered men with monstrous erections leering at her and shouting profanities. She awoke feeling agitated, clammy, like she'd narrowly escaped an encounter with a Texas rattler. What brought that on, she wondered. Maybe the lack of sex. How long had it been anyway? Could this have anything to do with seeing Phil Sanders again yesterday?

The rap at the door jolted Maggie. Coffee splashed over the rim of her mug onto her fingers. She licked them off quickly. Folding the pink furry wrap closed about her throat, she retied the belt before opening the door.

"Morning, Pop," Maggie greeted him with a smile, leaning forward to plant a kiss on her father's whiskered cheek. "Forget to shave this morning?" she joked, patting his prickly face.

"No, your mom was still sleeping. She had a restless night, so I didn't want to disturb her," he said as he sank into the chair opposite Maggie's. "Thanks, Maggie," he sighed, taking the steaming mug she offered. "She overdid it again yesterday. She got the fool notion to start spring cleaning." His weather-worn face was lined with concern. "By the time I got home, she'd finished the kitchen cupboards, had the curtains washed and a tuna casserole in the oven. It was almost like old times, except she paid for it all night. She has such a helluva time accepting that she needs to take it easy," he said, rubbing his stubbled chin. With Maggie he felt safe revealing his anxiety.

They had always been able to talk easily. This talking regularly with her father was one unexpected benefit Maggie deeply appreciated since moving home.

"She must have been feeling pretty good to even attempt such a task," Maggie speculated. She picked up her mug, taking a swallow. "She's just trying to get back to normal. She doesn't want us worrying about her all the time. Her check-up last month was a relief. There was no sign of cancer. The radiation seems to have taken care of anything left after surgery. Relax, Pop. Enjoy what is."

She reached over and gently rubbed his forearm, feeling the coarseness of the hair and the strength of his muscled arm. "I'll stop by later today when I come back from Joan's place. She has a house full with all Wayne's family home. I made a pan of brownies and a pot of beef barley soup that I thought she could use. I'll save some for you and Mom. Okay?"

He nodded.

"Now how about breakfast?" she asked, heading for the kitchen. "An omelet?"

"Sounds good. I'll make the toast," he offered, following her into the kitchen. He reached out and patted her hand as he'd done when she was a girl, to reassure both of them.

CHAPTER THREE

Joan and Wayne Sanders lived in the new subdivision, Pine Grove, overlooking the original part of town. The streets were wide and lined with mature pines, left by a forward-thinking developer. It was every kid's favorite place to gather pinecones for Christmas crafts. The school, two blocks away, was within walking distance for Max and Jessie.

Their home, in the middle of the block, was distinguished from the others by its russet brick gateposts, matching the trim on their creamy-colored bungalow. The flowerbeds, a blaze of reds, yellows and blues during the summer months, were immaculate, as were the lawns. No weed dared to raise its head before either Joan or Wayne sentenced it to death.

Max and Jessie had their assigned corner of the garden, where they could experiment with a variety of seeds and intriguing plants.

One year it was vegetable spaghetti. They watched in awe as the green mass outgrew their assigned patch and crept over the fence. Mrs. Clements, the next-door neighbor, was shocked when she discovered football-sized yellow orbs hanging on her raspberry canes. In autumn they marched up and down the street, offering for sale the fruits of their labors – three wheelbarrows worth.

The next year they tried growing popcorn with limited success, but their favorite was sunflowers, towering, sturdy and tall, overlooking the garden. With Wayne's help to harvest them, the neighborhood birds gorged themselves throughout the winter on their homegrown sunflower seeds. This Sanders family was definitely one with green thumbs.

Maggie took a deep breath to calm her fluttering butterflies as she rang the bell of Joan and Wayne's home. They'd been raising havoc in her stomach since she got up this morning, knowing she might see Phil again. She had resolved not to become involved with any man, much less Phil Sanders. She reasoned that her stomach's reaction to thoughts of Phil was like the hives she got when she ate too many strawberries – a reaction only, and not a welcome one.

With the soup pot tucked securely into a wicker basket surrounded by outdated issues of *The Nipawin Journal*, and the brownie pan in the other hand, she waited for someone to open the door. Finally, it opened a crack and one big blue eye appeared. Recognizing Maggie, Jessie, pulled it open further. She was wearing her 101 Dalmatians pajamas, tendrils of hair escaping from yesterdays' braids. "Dad, it's Maggie, an… and she's got a picnic basket. Come and see," she yelled over her shoulder.

"A picnic basket? In March? This I must see for myself." Instead of Wayne, whom Maggie was expecting, Phil, in well-worn baggy black sweats, filled the doorway. He studied her momentarily, thinking she looked as refreshing as the first tulip in spring. "Here, let me give you a hand," he offered, taking the basket, leading the way to the kitchen.

"Be careful, it's hot. Just off the stove, in fact," Maggie cautioned. She set the brownies on the counter, glancing around Joan's familiar sunlit peach and white kitchen. It was as neat as usual.

Suddenly self-conscious of his just-up appearance, Phil stammered, "J-Joan and Aunt Clara went uptown for a few minutes. They said they wouldn't be long. Joan needed a few things." He raked his hair and rubbed his chin, hoping she wouldn't judge him by his appearance at the moment, and if she did, that she wouldn't hold it against him. "What's in here?" he asked as a whiff from the basket registered.

Wayne appeared before she could answer. "Morning, Maggie. It is still morning, isn't it?" He reassured himself by a glance at the kitchen clock. "Here, let me take your coat. Have a seat. Will you have coffee?" he asked as he reached for her jacket. He hung it on the closet doorknob.

"I brought a couple of things, thinking maybe Joan could use them with the extra people around. Some soup and brownies." Maggie glanced at Phil, then turned again to Wayne. "Your Dad went so quickly. It's not something most people are prepared for. I'll have a quick coffee, if I'm not disturbing anything."

Little did she know how much she was disturbing him, Phil thought. A bolt of sexual awareness lurched straight to his loins when he'd seen her standing on the doorstep so calm and composed. He watched her as she slid behind the table, pushing it out slightly to be more comfortable. She looked like a store-wrapped gift, all neat and tidy, not a hair out of place. A rather large package for his liking, but definitely attractive. Maybe it was the independence she exuded that stirred his interest. Hell, no! He must be crazy, he told himself.

Wayne brought three mugs to the table. "You're not interrupting anything important. We were playing Tank Wars with Max on the computer. In fact, you might have saved Phil here from being blown to bits," he joked as he poured the coffee.

Phil grinned across the table at Maggie. "I'm at a disadvantage here," he explained to Maggie. "I have better things to do with my computer than play games. Besides, I've never heard of Tank Wars before. It's a silly game."

"It's okay, little brother. You always were a bit slow at catching on to some things." Wayne ruffled Phil's hair, patted his head patronizingly, and sat down.

Maggie nearly burst into laughter watching this exchange. Wayne, though two years older than Phil, was much smaller in stature. He had the look of a professor, his glasses sliding down his nose and his hairline receding. Phil took the teasing good-naturedly, considering he could without much effort have hurled his brother through the patio door and into the snow bank beyond.

"What a low blow! It doesn't deserve a reply," he scowled. Turning his attention to Maggie, Phil inquired, "Did you say you brought brownies?"

She nodded.

"Maybe we could sample them," he suggested hopefully.

The mention of the word brownies brought Max and Jessie racing into the kitchen, chanting, "Brownies! Brownies! Please, Dad, can we have some?"

Before Wayne had a chance to reply, Phil swept both of them up into his arms. "We should sample them, don't you think?" he asked.

They nodded in agreement. Jessie threw her arms around Phil's neck and planted a noisy kiss on his cheek. With one child on each knee, he pulled them together on his chest and rubbed his unshaven chin over their faces.

The squeals and squirming elicited by the tickling brought a smile to Maggie's face. It was delightful to see a man so at ease and comfortable with children, especially those not his own. She liked that. Children suited him.

"Okay, okay, enough already. One brownie," Wayne conceded. "It'll soon be lunch time." The playing stopped abruptly. All three nodded in agreement with Wayne.

"Maggie, you sure make good brownies," complemented Max, taking a big chewy bite. Phil and Jessie's heads wagged agreement in unison.

Here is a woman who can cook, thought Phil – something he could appreciate.

CHAPTER FOUR

Maggie was setting the bowls and spoons on the blue checkered tablecloth in her childhood home, only half listening to her mom chatter about her cleaning efforts of the previous day. Maggie had arrived with the promised pot of soup in time for lunch.

She was feeling warmed by the easy, friendly way Phil's family were with each other. Her own family was somewhat subdued in recent years – partly due to her Mom's illness. The noisy, boisterous behavior quieted to a hushed shuffle whenever they were together now. The children were often reminded, "Quiet, Grandma is resting."

"It feels good to have some of the winter's dust gone," her mom said. "It's three years since I've been able to do it myself, and it feels good," she reinforced, serving the soup.

Jackson Mills gently squeezed his wife's shoulder as he slid into the chair next to her. He was not quite used to the feel of her thinner body. Her more robust shape had represented Lenore's good health and even temperament to him all the forty-four years he'd known her. "Who was tossing and turning most of the night? That feels good?" he questioned teasingly.

"I'm just out of practice. I used muscles that haven't had a workout in a while, that's all," Lenore retorted, straightening her shoulders and pushing a strand of hair behind her ear. Changing the subject, she tasted the soup gingerly. "This is delicious, Maggie."

Maggie watched her parents with a new appreciation. They really enjoyed each other's company. She had no memories of them ever fighting, only her mother's sullen silences that would last about three days when they disagreed. During those rare times, her father found dozens of chores to do that would keep him busy and out of Lenore's range.

Maggie recalled only one vicious verbal argument years ago. It

19

was like a brush fire – blazed out of control and then died down, fooling everyone that the worst was over, only to be fanned again and again into roaring flames that seared every member of the family. The dilemma at the heart of the argument was whether or not her father should buy his own truck or continue to drive for Greyline Trucking. In the end, her father's wishes prevailed; he got his own rig, and neither one of them ever really regretted his decision. Only the memory of the battle remained.

His company, Mills Trucking, was moderately successful, employing Jackson and Fran Nelson, his part time bookkeeper.

Jackson Mills worked long hours to provide the necessities of life for his family. Lenore worked part time at Niles Ladies Wear after Don, their youngest son, started school. Maggie's brother Jonathon was three years older than she was, so it became their joint responsibility to watch Don after school until Lenore finished work. Lenore's wages bought the extras, like new bikes, summer camps and the trip to Montreal when Maggie was thirteen.

Jonathon, Maggie, and Don still talked about taking the subway to Olympic Stadium to watch the Expos, the delicious ball park hot dogs, and the horse and carriage ride through old Montreal by moonlight.

Maggie realized that her parents had the kind of relationship she had hoped for someday – respectful, fun, and comfortable. But, since Richard's exit from her life, Maggie had readjusted her thinking. Not everybody was supposed to be married with children. Since that didn't seem to be in the cards for her, she would enjoy what she did have.

Her mom's diagnosis shook her dad to his roots. Normally he was the strong one, but the thought of losing his companion of forty years cut off his strength at the knees.

It was a Saturday in May, nearly two years ago, that changed the direction of Maggie's life dramatically. She was curled up on a cushioned chaise, engrossed in Sidney Sheldon's *Memories of Midnight*. She was only remotely aware of the scent of the bursting purple hyacinths in cedar tubs next to her on the balcony or the freshly mowed grass in the park across the street. The mellow sounds of Neil Diamond drifted through the patio door. The ringing of the phone dragged her back to reality.

"Maggie, your mom found out yesterday that she has breast cancer," choked her dad. He took a quick breath and continued, "We would like you to come home for a while, if you could. It would mean a lot to your mom and me."

Maggie's life changed instantly with that phone call. She agonized over quitting her steno job at Ecco Heating Products in Saskatoon to return home to Nipawin. She knew her father would never have asked her to make such a sacrifice unless the situation was serious or he believed he couldn't handle it himself. Jackson Mills was a proud and capable man, husband and father. Maggie had never known a time when he'd crumbled, till now.

She anguished over giving up her job. It provided the only stability Maggie had known in recent years – stability and security she badly needed. Her life was just getting back on track after the last derailment.

The memory of that horrendous phase of her life flooded back. Her fiancé, Richard, had disappeared one day six years earlier, leaving Maggie's world a shattered mess. He left behind a good-bye note, a three thousand-dollar Visa bill and two pairs of holey socks.

Maggie was left to face friends and families and cancel their wedding arrangements.

She wished she would die, but instead she howled uncontrollably for three days, slept for the next three and was depressed for ten months.

Her only attempt at maintaining some kind of a normal life was forcing herself to go to work each day. For those few hours, her life had structure, a purpose.

Her best friend, Eileen, came to her rescue time after time. "Let's go to a movie… Drop in after work. We'll order Chinese… Doug's out of town so why don't we go to the theatre?"

"No thanks. I don't feel up to it," became Maggie's standard reply.

Finally Eileen suggested counseling with a therapist she knew from her work at the Crisis Centre. Reluctantly, Maggie dragged herself to that first appointment. Nancy, the therapist Eileen had recommended, helped her rediscover her will to live which Richard's abandonment had nearly snuffed out. She realized there was more to life than Richard. Slowly, over the months of talking and talking and talking, she regained her spark. She was okay, attractive but not beautiful, a robust woman who would have been treated like a goddess in Rembrandt's era.

After months of therapy, Maggie felt stable. But she decided she'd been hurt enough, so she wouldn't risk it again. Who needed a husband and kids anyway? A full, rich life was possible without them. She would take a greater interest in her niece and nephew. She developed a stronger bond with her brother Don's kids, Amanda and Michael. Their accepting preschool innocence soothed her bruised soul.

She kept them on weekends when Don and his wife Judy went to Banff skiing or shopping or just out for an evening. Maggie took them to the animal farm, the park, skating and swimming. They sat on the floor, eating popcorn, riveted to the Lion King, three times one Saturday evening.

During the tough months following Lenore's surgery and radiation therapy, Jackson relied heavily on Maggie. He counted on Maggie to interpret what the doctors said and explain it to him in plain English. Maggie was his sole confidante. With her, he could give voice to his worries and fears and shed a few tears if he felt compelled to do so. The exchange was not totally one-sided. Maggie did her share of worrying, wallowing and weeping while her father supported her. Mutual respect and caring forged a bond neither anticipated but both appreciated.

Lenore, Maggie's mother, handled the situation with what appeared to be a calm acceptance, sharing little with Jackson or her children. Maggie and her father tried talking to her about what was happening or likely to happen, but Lenore chose to keep her concerns to herself. They often found her absorbed in prayer, meditating or reading.

Now that the crisis was past, they had picked up the threads of their lives again somewhat tentatively. Jackson and Maggie took their cue from Lenore, and she wanted life back to normal, the way it was before cancer struck.

Maggie noticed her parents were more affectionate with each other, kinder. Observing them warmed her heart, but it also struck a sad note. It made her acutely conscious of the lack of someone special in her own life. Then she would tell herself that she had much to be grateful for – a loving family, a job she liked, the community in which she grew up and was comfortable.

When Maggie came home two years ago, she'd moved back into her old bedroom. Her mom had redecorated it since Maggie had left, but it still felt safe and secure, like home. She stayed until her mom was feeling stronger. The day her mother ordered her out of the kitchen was the day Maggie began looking for her own place, popping in every day to do the heavier chores. They both appreciated having their own space again.

A chance meeting with Joan Sanders in the produce department of the Co-op store one evening proved to be rewarding. They reminisced over coffee and got caught up on the events of each other's lives. Maggie recounted how her life in the city was halted suddenly by her mother's illness. She saved the broken engagement story for later. Maggie knew Joan had married Wayne Sanders, but she had heard nothing of her since. She learned that Joan and Wayne had two children. Max was five and Jessie was three. She worked as the accounting clerk at Tobin Lake Motors.

Joan asked her if she would be interested in a job. Their receptionist, Jackie Renard, was going on maternity leave. Joan was excited about the idea and her eagerness was infectious. Maggie applied the next day and started the following week. To Maggie, this was all temporary, until she could move back to Saskatoon.

She missed the anonymity of the city, the rush of life around her, the wide choice of activities. Then the receptionist on leave asked for an additional six months leave of absence after her maternity leave was up. Maggie had been at Tobin Lake Motors for nearly a year now. Jackie had decided last week not to return, so the job was Maggie's permanently if she wanted it. She had a week to make a decision. With Joan's father-in-law's dying and all the resulting confusion, Maggie had given it little thought – till now.

"Earth calling Maggie." A voice reached Maggie's consciousness. She realized her mom and dad were both staring at her. "Welcome back. Where were you?" asked Lenore.

"Sorry. I was thinking about something," she replied, pushing her bowl toward the middle of the table, leaning forward, crossing her arms in front of her. Taking a breath, she forged ahead. "Jackie Renard has decided to quit and stay home with her baby. I have to decide if I want her job permanently."

"You like it there, don't you?" asked Jackson, his eyes wide in surprise. He liked having Maggie in town and had come to rely on her in many ways. He hadn't considered Maggie moving, especially since she had a good job.

"Sure, it's okay, but I always thought I would go back to Saskatoon as soon as you could manage on your own again, Mom."

Lenore shot her husband a look that halted any more questions. "You know that I am fine now, Maggie. I appreciate everything that you have done for me, but if that's what you want to do, please don't let us stop you. You need to do what is right for you." She reached over and brushed Maggie's cheek lightly with the back of her hand.

"That's the problem. Now that the time has come, I'm not so certain." She had anticipated a negative reaction from her dad. She would miss their cozy Saturday morning breakfasts that had become a routine they both looked forward to in the past months. Her mother was anxious to prove her ability to be independent, but Maggie sensed that she would miss the closeness they had shared during her illness. She was grateful for the more mature relationship that had developed between them. But a decision would have to be made soon.

CHAPTER FIVE

The brilliant sunshine streaming through the east-facing window warmed Maggie's bedroom, forcing her out of bed earlier than she had planned on Sunday morning. It promised to be a glorious spring day. Maggie loved Sunday morning – in particular breakfast. It was her treat of the week – toasted bagels with butter and honey. Coffee and the newspaper made it a luxuriously relaxing, almost sensual, beginning to her day.

She knew that her self-imposed celibacy could reduce her life to a barren, mundane existence unless she chose to make some occasions extraordinary. And so began her nurturing Sunday ritual. The breakfast was often followed by attending church services.

Sunday was her day to catch up on the numerous chores she neglected during the week, laundry, dusting, vacuuming, letter writing. Dressed in well-worn grey sweats, her hair pulled back with an emerald green hairband to match her Roughriders T-shirt, her stereo blaring her favorite Celine Dion CD, Maggie attacked her apartment with a dust cloth and vacuum cleaner.

Dusting and cleaning her collected possessions, turning them over in her hands, always brought back memories of what made each precious to her. Her bell collection occupied several shelves of the tall oak corner curio cabinet. She picked up her first bell – the one with the Expos logo that she picked up in Montreal years ago. All the others were gifts from family and friends. Her friends Eileen and Doug brought her the brass bell from the Black Forest in Germany. The crystal bell Jonathon gave her on her twenty-first birthday. The delicate bell with the ceramic chipmunk she had received in the office gift exchange her last Christmas at Ecco Heating. They were spread out on the coffee table while she dusted the shelves. Maggie was planning a new arrangement in the cabinet when the doorbell chimed.

Thinking it might be her father, Maggie gasped when she opened the door and there stood Phil, grinning from ear to ear. He carried her picnic basket containing her empty soup pot and cake pan. Suddenly self-conscious about her appearance, the red blotches beginning at her neck moved slowly toward her face. "Oh, Phil." Smoothing her hair down, she motioned him in with her dust cloth in hand.

Phil's discomfort at being asked to run errands for Joan dissolved when Maggie opened the door looking nothing like the elegant woman he'd met at his father's funeral or the immaculately groomed one who brought the soup and brownies yesterday. The expression pulled up the corners of his mouth to reveal those deadly dimples. His eyes were instinctively drawn to the hanks of deeply bronzed hair standing up behind the hairband. His grin spread across his face until he broke into an uncontrollable laugh.

The blotches from her neck raced up over her face to the tips of hair standing on end. "I wasn't expecting company," she snapped, annoyed that he was laughing at her. A quick glance in the mirror over the hall table revealed a rather comical image. She couldn't help but smile at the sight. She removed the hairband, ran her fingers through her mop to bring some semblance of order. She noticed the crimson hue of her cheeks.

Phil was immediately embarrassed about making Maggie feel ill at ease. "I'm sorry I've caught you at a bad time," he apologized, handing her the picnic basket.

"It's not a bad time. I was just cleaning." Not wanting him to leave just yet, she added, "It's time for a break anyway. Got time for coffee?"

"Sure." He followed her into the kitchen, noting the bright, cheery yellow and white decor.

Maggie set the basket on the counter and busied herself making coffee. Flipping the switch on, she turned to find him staring out the window over the dining table into the branches of the stately pines. "Have a seat. Excuse me for a second. I'll be right back." She disappeared around the corner. Celine Dion went from a roar to a whisper as she turned the volume down on her way to the bathroom.

Phil sat at the table, amazed at the bird's eye view this window provided. He spotted a pair of robins sitting side by side deep in the sanctuary of the branches. They were the first robins he'd observed this spring.

Maggie found him like that, a few minutes later, elbows on the table, his chin resting on his knuckles, watching the pantomime in the pine boughs. She had brushed her hair and applied a bit of mascara on her lashes. "I see you've spotted Harry and Florence. What are they up to today?" Maggie brought two mugs of steaming coffee to the table. Placing one in front of Phil, she pulled out the chair at right angles to him for herself. She was grateful that she had bought such big cushioned chairs. Diminutive chairs left grooves on the sides of her thighs, not to mention occasionally getting stuck in them. Her choice suited Phil's generous size also.

"A lively discussion on nest design," Phil replied with authority. "What a great view, so peaceful and serene, except for the chatter." He noticed the change in her appearance. "Why Harry and Florence?" he inquired, pointing at the birds.

"He looks a little tough and gruff on the outside but is really a softie inside, like a Harry. He reminds me of Clint Eastwood's Dirty Harry. Now, Florence, on the other hand, makes me think of a neighbor we had when I was a kid. Maybe you remember Florence Watson?" Maggie asked.

Phil thought for a moment, then nodded.

Maggie continued, "She's delicate and fragile, but it's a front for her inner strength. She also knows just how to manipulate Harry without his realizing what happened to him. Definitely a Florence," she said, absorbed by the drama. Just then Florence nuzzled up to Harry and briefly tucked her head under his wing.

"You're right. She does know how to handle him." Phil's smile showed off his nearly even, strong white teeth. His dancing coffee-colored eyes swept across the tidy u-shaped yellow and white kitchen, the two childish drawings pinned to the fridge with lemon magnets. "This is nice." He relaxed, leaning back into the plush upholstery. "This feels like an oasis compared to the chaos at Wayne's house." He threw up a hand before she could respond. "Don't get me wrong. They are great kids, just that I'm not used to that kind of craziness."

"I know exactly. I have a niece and a nephew that I adore – Michael and Amanda. They are always so busy that it feels like a whirlwind blew through the place, leaving me exhausted. It's a relief when they go home and my space is my own again. But I really enjoy them when I do see them. They have a way of making me forget everything for a little while." Slightly embarrassed by this admission, Maggie shifted her attention to the methodical nest-building activities.

Phil picked up Maggie's discomfort and decided against pursuing the matter. He was reminded that he too had suffered some wounds to this point in his life, some of which were still a bit tender. For some reason, he had never considered that the same was true for Maggie. He'd lived with the idea that big women were the jolly, happy-go-lucky, roll-with-the-punches sort who could laugh off any hurt and carry on defiantly. At this very moment, she looked vulnerable and fragile, making Phil want to reach out to reassure her that he understood. Instead, he sat frozen, the words jammed in his throat.

Recovering her poise, Maggie turned her gaze back to her guest. "Joan tells me you teach at Carlton. What subjects?"

"English and Physical Education." He explained how one complemented the other and helped destroy the stereotypes involved – that a jock could think past the next play on the field and that a scholar wasn't necessarily a wimp with spectacles riding low on his nose.

His first position had been in Glaslyn, population four hundred, junior high and all the coaching he could handle – volleyball, football, track and field. The football team, the Glaslyn Gladiators, went to the semi-finals in the unit during his second year there. Then it was four years at Royal in North Battleford and two at Pace Comprehensive in Regina. Three years ago, he felt the north calling him. He missed the forest, the lakes, being able to leave the world behind within half an hour and be dropping a hook in the water. That's how he came to Carlton in Prince Albert. Teaching was still a thrill and a challenge. The bonus was that he was only an hour and a half from home, his dad, Wayne and Joan and the kids. Ron and Kathy in Saskatoon were about the same distance. It was ideal.

Phil kept to the statistics, carefully avoiding any reference to either Sandra or Shelley. "How about you?" he asked after a moment, peering at Maggie over the rim of his mug. He noticed she had the most captivating deep blue eyes. They suggested a depth of emotion and sensitivity.

"After high school, I went to Robertson Business College in Saskatoon but couldn't find a clerical job, so I spent four years in the children's wear department at The Bay, hating every minute of it. I watched the 'Help Wanted' section in the paper and applied for those jobs that sounded interesting. Finally, I got a call from Ecco Heating. After the interview, I wasn't so sure that I wanted the job but decided to give it a try. I was there ten years, till Mom got cancer, and I came back here. End of story, not very exciting," Maggie concluded. She had steered clear of any mention of Richard. Both were aware that discussion of personal entanglements had been circumvented.

He really wanted to ask her about her personal relationships, about whether or not she was seeing someone, but he decided against it. She might consider his probing rude and out of line. They were just barely acquainted. He settled for more neutral territory. The personal stuff would wait till another time – and another time there would be, as far as Phil was concerned. He was drawn to Maggie as a moth to a porch light in summer.

"Joan told me about your mother. How is she doing?"

"Good. She's a real fighter," Maggie laughed. She recounted how the recent cleaning episode was typical of her feisty nature and how her father worried.

"Sounds like you get along okay with your folks. I had a pretty good relationship with my dad too. Maybe it's natural to have regrets after someone dies," he said, looking up from his coffee. The sadness was evident in the deep brown eyes. He hesitated, then continued, "I wish I had made more of an effort to spend time with him these past years since I've been in P.A."

Tiny lines appeared across his tanned brow. Maggie had the urge to gently smooth them with her finger. "When people go quickly without warning like your dad did, there is no time to prepare, make amends or say good-bye. I'm sorry about your dad, Phil. He was a real gentleman." She stopped, wondering whether to risk sharing with him a conclusion she had reached. In this moment, despite his bulk, he looked fragile. She'd risk it.

"I had lots of time to think about things like that when Mom was ill. I've learned regrets are a waste of time and energy. It's more rewarding to spend that energy doing something about things I can change."

Phil nodded, knowing the truth in her words. They turned their attention to Florence and Harry in a contemplative comfortable silence. The flurry of construction progressed under their watchful eyes.

As Phil was leaving, he lingered in the doorway, shifting from one foot to the other like a sixteen-year-old, dying to ask for the family car for the first time. "W-w-would you mind if I called you sometime?" he stammered. "To check on Florence and Harry?" he added quickly, not wanting to admit how he'd enjoyed their conversation.

"Sure, anytime," Maggie replied. She closed the door and leaned against the back of it, wondering why she had agreed so readily. Joan had told her about Phil's many women – tiny and slender. She was certain he would never call her. He had asked to call just to be polite. She almost convinced herself that her reply had been a simple courtesy, nothing more. Besides, she was not about to trust those chestnut eyes.

CHAPTER SIX

The snowbanks, which were piled high onto the generous boulevards running down the centre of Main Street, disappeared into tiny rivers and lakes as the sun's warmth grew stronger. March turned to April. Children wearing rubber boots and armed with sticks navigated makeshift crafts along the streets and ditches on the edge of town. Wet feet were often the result of an overturned raft or slippery footing. The freedom of spring was temporarily interrupted four times by swift, sharp snowstorms.

The last vicious attack of winter occurred at the beginning of April. The gusting winds that accompanied the six inches of snow created unusual and picturesque banks and cliffs along the edge of the carragana hedge that bordered Woodlawn cemetery. Only the children seemed to notice, taking advantage of another opportunity to design and construct snow sculptures of varying refinement. Feeling assaulted physically and emotionally by the unpredictability of nature, most folks retreated to the warmth and security of their homes. Joan said she planned to pick up a couple of movies as they hurried from work to their cars blanketed in white.

Perhaps the decision to stay in Nipawin was a mistake, Maggie thought. A cloud of gloominess settled over her as the storm clouds unleashed a blast of winter outside. From her living room window, she watched what little traffic there was crawl cautiously along the highway coming into town from Codette and Tisdale in the south. Usually, Maggie enjoyed her solitude, but tonight, she was unsettled and roamed from room to room. She thought about other women she knew. She imagined them securely cocooned against the elements with their families. She was more aware than ever that she was alone. She fantasized about what it would feel like to have someone to snuggle with and watch a movie. Joan was lucky, she decided.

Maggie mentally ticked off the list of friends she could call. She dialed Eileen's number.

Maggie had come to count on Eileen's listening ear. She was her sounding board. Eileen knew the right questions to ask, so that she could see things more clearly in her own mind. This restlessness had saturated her being, but the root cause wouldn't pop to the surface. Her need to talk to Eileen became almost desperate as she listened to the phone ring the fifth time.

"What's up, Maggie?"

"Just wanted to talk to you, Eileen. Nothing special, really."

"Okay, Maggie. What's going on? That tone of voice doesn't fool me." Eileen cut to the chase when Maggie failed to pinpoint the source of her discomfort. A pause, and then she asked, "Would this have anything to do with a guy? Have you met someone, Maggie?"

"Of course not. Don't be silly. You know how I feel about getting involved again."

"You protest too much. Who is he? Let's hear it."

And so Maggie told her about Phil. "But he hasn't called. It's been weeks." She was trying to keep the discouragement out of her voice.

"So call him."

"I can't do that!"

"Why not? Sometimes you have to risk what is for what could be."

There was a moment's silence while Maggie pondered.

"It's your choice, Maggie, as always."

She could not call Phil. She had never in her life called a guy and she wasn't about to begin now. She paced. She tried reading. Phil's face, complete with his devilish grin, skipped unheeded through her mind. She wondered what he was doing on such a blustery evening.

Risk what is, Eileen had said. What was so great about her present circumstances anyway that they couldn't stand to be improved? Before she could talk herself out of it, Maggie dialed his number. Her stomach quivered and tightened as she waited. It rang four, five, six times...

"Hello," a breathless, high-pitched female voice answered on the other end of the line. "Hello," she repeated when there was no reply.

Stunned, Maggie recovered enough to stammer, "I-I think I have the w-wrong number. S-Sorry."

"Who are you trying to reach?"

"I-I was calling Phil Sanders."

"Right number, but he's unavailable at the moment. Can I take a message?" the voice asked politely.

"No, that's fine. B-Bye." Maggie dropped the phone into its cradle as though it was a red-hot poker.

Maggie berated herself during the remainder of the evening for acting without forethought. How could she be so stupid? To just call a man she hardly knew. He had a girlfriend. Maybe she lived with him for all she knew. It was à good thing Phil didn't answer. That would have been very embarrassing. What a close call! Well, at least now she knew he was attached and could stop daydreaming about him being somehow different than other guys she'd known. She must have read him wrong. Despite his immense size, he appeared to have a relaxed, gentle, fun-loving nature. And those rich brown eyes that seemed to see right through her. He was bad news – best left alone!

Easter was late in April, and Maggie was looking forward to the break. The entire Mills family would be together. Maggie had been shopping for treats for the Easter egg hunt, which was the family tradition after church service Sunday morning. Helping her mother plan for the holiday helped to distract her from the restlessness she felt as winter finally eased into spring.

There were still a few stubborn snowbanks under shrubs and along the north side of the buildings. The air smelled of sunshine. Tulips and crocuses with a southern exposure were bravely poking their heads out toward the warming sun. The birds of summer had returned, sending up a chorus of sound to greet her every morning through her open bedroom window. Maggie hung a hummingbird feeder in the pine outside her window.

It took ten days, but finally she spotted the gleaming green of a male hummingbird one morning as she put the coffee on. The sunlight reflecting off his back was a brilliant emerald green. He looked dressed for a formal party with his ruby-colored necktie and black top hat as he nervously sampled the nectar. The female appeared next. The pair became daily visitors. Maggie was anxious for Easter to arrive, so she could show them off to Michael and Amanda.

It had been four weeks since she'd seen Phil and not a word. Maggie wasn't surprised. She was convinced that he never really intended to call. It was just a line. Just as well. It saved the heartache when things didn't work out.

Phil's dimpled smile haunted her daydreams and nighttime dreams as well. What would it feel like to put her arms around his burly frame? Let his hair slip through her fingers. Without warning such images would pop into her mind, and it took conscious effort to push them aside. She wondered if he would be coming to town for Easter. Joan hadn't mentioned it, and Maggie refused to ask. They wished each other a Happy Easter after work on the Thursday before the holiday weekend.

The phone rang, breaking Maggie's concentration. She picked it up carefully; trying not to get it all smeared with chocolate.

"Please come over to Gramma's place, Auntie. We just got here and I asked Gramma if I could phone you. Please, Auntie!" Michael begged. Hardly stopping to catch his breath, he continued, "Uncle Jon is here too, and he said we could play a game or watch a video – whatever we want. When are you coming, Auntie?"

Maggie dropped the last chocolate-coated marshmallow Easter eggs onto the cookie sheet. She'd found the recipe in the last issue of *Chatelaine*. It looked time-consuming and piddly – just the project she'd needed this evening as she'd thought about the empty hours ahead. Now she glanced at the clock, astonished at the lateness.

"You are coming over, aren't you, Auntie? Please, please," he implored.

"It's kinda late, Michael."

"We slept nearly all the way here, so we aren't a bit tired. Mom said we could stay up late. Will you come?"

"Okay, I'll be there in a few minutes," Maggie agreed. The pots and utensils were quickly dumped into the sink and a quick swipe across the counter would suffice till tomorrow. She popped a sample of her new creation into her mouth, tossed her apron into the pantry, grabbed her keys, and out the door she went. Maggie was as anxious to see Michael and Amanda as they were to see her.

Jonathon had dug out their ancient Snakes and Ladders game. "I'm surprised that you even remembered this game, Jon. What a great idea." She congratulated him with a ruffle of his always unruly, much-hated curls.

Neither Michael nor Amanda had seen the game before. Maggie and Jonathon – called Jon by nearly everyone except his mother – taught the children to play their favorite childhood game. Don and Judy visited with Jackson and Lenore in the comfortable, lived-in living room.

Near midnight, Michael won his first game, accompanied by backslapping and high-fives. He said he wasn't going to bed until he won one game. Amanda was too tired to care as Don carried her off to bed. A triumphant Michael followed.

Wishing everyone a good night, Maggie headed for home across town, driving through the nearly deserted streets. Only a few sporty types were still cruising Main Street. Waiting at the traffic lights, a red Mustang pulled up beside her. The driver gunned his engine as though he were about to begin the Indy 500. She glanced over at the young male, wearing his baseball cap backwards. He was taking advantage of the time at the red light to nuzzle the blonde sitting beside him. As the light turned green, the Mustang rocketed forward, the driver's lips still clamped onto the girl's face. Her attention was so claimed by the amazing feat of the Mustang's driver that Maggie nearly missed the sea-blue Jimmy passing by her in the intersection. A quick glance at the driver made her heart skip a beat. It was Phil. Judging from the way his eyes followed her, it was obvious that he'd seen her too.

Watching her rearview mirror as she proceeded, Maggie saw the Jimmy brake, make a U-turn in the middle of the abandoned street, race through the traffic light and up behind her. In her rearview mirror, she could see Phil motioning for her to pull over. She stopped in front of Tobin Lake Motors. He pulled in behind her. Maggie took a deep breath, forcing herself to exhale as she watched him approach in her side mirror. She had no time to think or plan her next move. He was right there, smiling broadly, showing off those gorgeous dimples.

He leaned on the door, poking his head into the window, barely inches from Maggie's face. "What a pleasant surprise."

Trying desperately to remain calm, Maggie replied, "Hello. Just getting into town?"

"Yes. I was planning to come tomorrow, then changed my mind about ten o'clock so threw some things together, and here I am." He straightened up and inhaled deeply, both hands rubbing his lower back.

Phil sensed her unease. It felt like they were back at square one, the day he'd called at her apartment. He'd let too much time pass. He should have called. He knew he had to act before she raced away or he changed his mind. He leaned into the window again and flashed his sexiest smile. "Can I buy you a coffee?"

CHAPTER SEVEN

With no all night coffee bars in Nipawin, going for coffee meant going to Maggie's apartment. She wished she'd taken the time to clean up her kitchen properly as she flipped on the light. On second thought, why worry. She would just approach this meeting with cool detachment, she resolved. After all, it was Phil who hadn't been interested enough to call. Why was she even bothering to see him now? A weak moment, she decided.

Phil hung his windbreaker on the closet doorknob and followed her into the kitchen. "Looks like you've been busy," Phil commented. Maggie, pouring water into the coffeemaker, turned around to see him licking chocolate off his finger. "Tastes good."

"Oops! I must have missed some. I was in a hurry to see my niece and nephew when I left. You'll have to excuse the mess." Maggie decided her less than spotless kitchen wasn't going to make her uncomfortable. She had no energy or inclination for putting on a façade. Besides, it didn't look like it was bothering Phil.

"It's nice to see a kitchen that looks used. What were you making?" He'd found another dollop of chocolate on the counter edge and again wiped it off with his finger. She felt his presence slightly unsettle her as he leaned against the counter watching her, savoring the sweet chocolate. How could licking chocolate off one's finger be so erotic, she wondered. Maggie was sure he had no idea just how sexy he appeared to her at the moment.

She felt his eyes travel up and down her generous frame. She wondered how he felt about what he saw. She was unsure about the meaning of the broad grin on his face when she turned around to face him. Was it amusement, amazement or approval?

Maggie explained about the chocolate marshmallow Easter eggs she'd made to surprise her niece and nephew.

Confusion was written all over his face as he tried to fathom the creation of a marshmallow egg. "Can you show me?" he asked.

She couldn't believe that he would be interested, but she humored him. Seeing his wide-eyed expression as she presented the results, Maggie knew he was impressed. Allowing him a taste test scored even bigger points.

"Here, let me pour the coffee," Phil offered as the dripping pot ceased gurgling and Maggie returned her creations to the fridge. He went straight to the cupboard near the fridge and took out two sunshine yellow mugs. Maggie liked a guy who paid attention to details, and it looked like Phil was one who did. At least he remembered where she kept her mugs, even if he couldn't remember to pick up the phone and call.

As he sat across the table from her, calmly chatting about school, Maggie wondered for the millionth time who the woman was who had answered his phone the night she'd foolishly called him. Why would he be here if he was in a relationship? Maybe he was one of those who liked a woman in every port.

Maggie's attention returned to what Phil was talking about. It seemed that he was feeling a bit guilty about not calling after all, judging from his lengthy explanation about how busy he'd been these past few weeks. He'd been spending more time with his friend Jason. Jason and his wife were going for marriage counseling, he explained. They had been trying unsuccessfully to have a baby and were now to the point where they were not even sure they wanted the marriage. He was Jason's sounding board.

Maggie's brow knit in concentration. Her mind kept wandering. Deciding suddenly that honesty was the safest route, Maggie blurted it out. "I called your place about three weeks ago, in the middle of a blizzard, and…"

Before she could finish, he exclaimed, "That was you! Why didn't you leave a message? Kathy told me someone had called. Ron and Kathy got stranded at my place overnight. You remember Ron, my brother? Ron and I were digging the snow out of the motor of his car about the time you called."

Maggie felt her face turn crimson from the neck of her sweatshirt up. She lowered her head and mumbled, "I thought it was your girlfriend." She looked up into those liquid brown eyes, staring at her in amazement. "I didn't want to interrupt anything." Squirming, she added defensively, "Besides, in case you have forgotten, you said you'd call me."

He had promised to call. He hadn't forgotten. He just kept putting it off. It wasn't a good time. He didn't know what to say. One week turned into two, and it became easier to push it into the recesses of his mind, a niggling thought he didn't want to confront. Saying he would call was a line he used casually with women. Seeing the challenge in the set of her jaw, he knew he would have to speak the truth to himself and to Maggie. Looking at her right here in front of him, he wondered why he had hesitated. He knew in his heart that if he got involved with this woman, she would challenge him. She looked confident and self-assured to him, but the tears welling up in her eyes betrayed her vulnerability.

"There is one thing I will ask of you, Phil. That's honesty. Let's not play games, okay," she said with more sinew than she felt. With her thumb she flicked away the tear that threatened to run down her cheek. She set her mug down, braced her elbows on the table with her chin resting on her folded hands, waiting for him to reply. The ball was now in his court – his move.

"Honesty, eh," he said, setting his mug on the table between them, intently studying its contents. His palms gripped the mug as though it might take flight if he didn't. He wasn't sure how he could put into words what he suspected. "I did say I would call, didn't I?" he admitted.

He looked up to see Maggie nodding gently, her chin still on her hands. Phil could see the muscles along her shoulders tighten slightly. Her eyes held his, challenging him to be truthful at last. He'd never met a woman like Maggie. She didn't dance around issues but faced them head on. He wasn't sure he knew how to handle her honesty. But then he hadn't fared well in the game playing department either, so what did he have to lose?

"I guess, the reason I didn't call was because I was afraid," he sighed quietly. He watched her face for a reaction. He detected a hint of puzzlement.

"Afraid." She sounded unconvinced. "Of what?"

"Of getting involved again." Now that he'd started, there was no turning back. She said she wanted the truth, so he would tell her as honestly as he could. He took a deep breath and continued, "I'm afraid to take that risk again. I'm not sure I have the energy to start all over. If I get involved with or care about someone again, it will change my whole life and I feel like I've just got it back in order. It's comfortable, predictable."

His rich brown eyes pleaded with her for a response of some kind – understanding, pity, curiosity, amusement – something.

Maggie was reminded of Lady, the Chesapeake pup they'd owned as kids, waiting for the fetch command. That look melted her heart as a kid. Now, gazing into those big brown eyes, she could feel her firmness fading slightly.

His gaze held hers. "I'm afraid of you," he stated.

CHAPTER EIGHT

Maggie was stunned. This confession was not what she had expected. She thought he might admit that he was involved with someone, that she was too fat to consider having a relationship with, or that she was just a diversion – for fun, or he was lonely, a one-night stand.

"Me! Why on earth would you be afraid of me?" She blinked twice to be sure this wasn't a bad dream. She'd never thought of herself as any more threatening than a gentle Saint Bernard pup.

"You're so direct and genuine. I feel comfortable talking to you, and that scares me. I was thinking about you as I was driving here tonight. Thinking of all the times I wanted to pick up the phone and ask you to go out and grab a cup of coffee or go for a walk, but you were ninety miles away. Then, when I saw you at the lights, it seemed like a sign of some kind. Sounds crazy, I know. Besides all that, my track record with women stinks. When I thought about it, I wasn't sure I wanted to try again." He paused, staring into her eyes with such intensity that Maggie could hardly doubt that this was the truth.

Phil slumped back into the chair; suddenly aware that he was attempting to crush the mug with his palms as he often did with empty beer cans. He released the mug gingerly and spread his tanned hands palms down on the tabletop. Slowly he exhaled deeply, relaxing, his gaze glued to his outstretched hands. He could hardly believe that he had actually vocalized the thoughts that had been racing around inside his head for weeks. Well, he thought, she asked for the truth, and that's what she got. It hadn't been as difficult as he'd imagined.

Slowly, timidly, Maggie reached across the distance between them, lightly brushing the back of his hand with her fingertips. His fingers, thick and blunt, were spread out, making his hands look the

41

size of dinner plates. The golden brown hairs sprouted on the back of his fingers, up the back of his hands and wrists, disappearing under his cuffs, were surprisingly soft beneath her touch. Then she returned her hands to grasp her mug. She reminded herself that what she felt was just a physical attraction.

"I'm not a radical feminist who devours men for lunch," she offered. A smile threatened at the corners of her mouth at the thought. She added, seriously, "I've had my share of failures, too. I understand your reluctance. It's not easy to take that risk again. I feel the same way. My head is telling me to stay clear."

Phil lifted his rich brown lashes to meet Maggie's gaze. The relief was obvious on Phil's features. The furrows on his brow eased, and the dimples reappeared. The slow smile showed off his strong, straight teeth, the laugh lines at the corners of those tempting brown eyes.

Turning his palms upward, he extended them across the table in invitation. Maggie responded hesitantly, slowly placing her hands in his. Phil closed his grasp gently over them, warm and solid. The notion that this was a woman worth holding onto crossed his mind.

"I'd like to get to know you better, Maggie. That I do know, even if I'm somewhat apprehensive. I've never known a woman like you."

"You mean, a woman as big as me," she stated flatly, needing to get the issue of her size out of the way.

"No, that's not what I meant. But, yes… that too." He squeezed her hands. "Both Sandra and Shelley were tiny. So were the other women I've dated. It seems I've developed a pattern that hasn't worked well. Maybe this is the time for a change."

He reluctantly released her hands and picked up his mug. With more coffee, Maggie's encouragement, and a few pertinent questions, Phil was grateful for the opportunity to talk about his life and loves.

During his first term at Glaslyn, he'd met Sandra at a convention in North Battleford. They were married the following year, after he obtained a job in North Battleford, where she taught kindergarten. Married less than two years, Sandra was killed in a car accident on her way to Regina to help her sister shop for her upcoming wedding. It seemed unreal. Sometimes he wondered if he'd ever been married, because the enduring pain overshadowed the short happy time they had together. Time only dulled his aching heart, so after three more years, he decided a geographical cure might be the answer.

In Regina, he met Shelley at a party at a staff member's home. She was cute and tiny, bubbly and impulsive, and incredibly sexy. She affected him like champagne. He quickly lost his balance and sense of reason. He found himself married within two months to a woman he barely knew. It lasted seven months. Arriving home earlier than usual, the result of a flu bug, he found Shelley in bed with a co-worker. Even though he knew the marriage was a mistake, Phil found it difficult to admit he'd screwed up, that he was twenty-nine years old, twice married, but still alone.

"I thought I would make a fresh start in P.A., but so far there have been no serious entanglements. Some casual dates, but nobody I wanted to spend time with... till now," he added cautiously. Phil couldn't believe how much lighter and freer he felt with this unburdening. A smile spread slowly across his mouth. "And maybe your size is an indication that we are compatible. Who knows? In case you haven't noticed," he said as he stretched his arms toward the ceiling, "I'm not exactly pint-sized myself."

Phil's admission of the obvious instigated a bout of laughter and eased the tension.

Feeling consoled and buoyed, Maggie shared, "I have noticed you aren't the string bean you were in high school."

"Nor are you the snob I thought you were back then. I think we've both changed since then."

CHAPTER NINE

"Would you like to go out to the park? I could borrow a thermos from Joan to take coffee with us, if you are interested."

Maggie, wrapped in a bright pink bath sheet, leaving wet footprints on the carpet, had grabbed the phone on its fifth ring. She had slept late. It was the Saturday of a holiday weekend. She wasn't planning to go to her parents' house till evening.

Friday, Good Friday had been a full day. Michael and Amanda were assigned the task of egg coloring. There were church services and an energetic game of Monopoly after the children were tucked in. Maggie began to yawn soon into the game. Jon had teased her, "What's with this yawning, sleepy-head?" She didn't bother to explain that she had only four hours of sleep because she'd been up talking with Phil till past four in the morning.

"Sounds like a plan. I could use some fresh air. I'm barely awake, so give me an hour. Is that okay with you?"

"Perfect!" purred a relieved Phil. "See you then."

Maggie's stomach did a little flip as she hung up the phone. He had said when he left early Friday morning that he would call. He assured her that he meant it this time. Only this time it was easy, he was only a few blocks away. What would happen when he was back in P.A., an hour and a half drive instead of five minutes?

The park was deserted. The picnic tables were still tipped up in their winter position to allow the melting snow to run off. They picked a site on the bank overlooking the river. The buds on the poplar trees were just bursting forth in a gentle new green. The spruce trees were a slightly darker shade. The first spring rains had washed away the menacing black winter pallor, leaving the air smelling newly scrubbed.

The gurgling powerful surge of the river below drew them to the

44

bank's edge. The floodgates of the power dam just a mile upstream from Nipawin controlled the Saskatchewan River's flow. The run off and warming sun had broken up the rotten ice last week. Through the clearing of an old path down to the water, they could see the last of the ice being carried away by the current like dumplings floating atop a chicken stew.

The old trail was steep and challenging under ideal summer conditions. Today, there were still remnants of snow along the path's edges. The melting snow coursing its way to the river gouged out the center of the path.

There was some heat in the bright sun. Maggie could feel it penetrating the layers of clothing she wore – a T-shirt, a sweatshirt and a fleece-lined jacket. The warmth spread from her shoulders and down her back. It made her feel like stretching up toward the source of the heat like a cat rising from a nap on a sunny window ledge to diffuse the heat to the tips of her limbs. A gust of raw, bone-chilling wind caught them, reminding them that old man winter had not yet given up his grip on this part of the country.

They righted a table, moving it to a spot protected by giant spruce trees. From the borrowed cooler, Phil brought forth a plastic blue tablecloth, a thermos, and two mugs. Reaching in again, he turned to her, beaming.

He reminded her of Michael, the day he proudly uncupped his hands to show her the treasure he'd found at the lake's edge – a frog the size of a quarter. Phil displayed a bag of hot dog buns and wieners. "I hope you're hungry. I brought lunch."

A blast of icy wind off the river found the tiny clearing. Maggie shivered, sipping the hot coffee. She watched Phil build a fire. They found a small pile of dry firewood under one of the picnic tables.

His broad shoulders strained the seams of the denim sheep-lined jacket as he bent over the infant flames. The blue and green plaid shirt was tucked into his jeans that stretched across his hips and backside. He looked like he belonged in jeans, more comfortable than in the suit he'd worn at his father's funeral. Maggie decided he was definitely easy to look at, as he tickled and teased the flames into the fullness of a fire.

From his pocket came a Swiss army knife. He cut and trimmed to

45

a sharp point two sticks from young poplar seedlings growing near the edge of the bank. They were perfect to roast the wieners.

"You're a regular Boy Scout." Maggie took the offered stick and skewered a wiener. She huddled close to the fire, carefully turning the meat over the dancing blaze.

Phil squatted near the fire to roast a wiener too. His shoulder was not quite touching hers, not an intimate closeness, but a friendly closeness.

Watching Maggie slowly, methodically turn the meat, he observed, "You look like an experienced hot-dog-cooker." At her playful expression, he explained, "That's a term I learned from Max last summer when we were camping. Do you like camping?"

"Our family went camping lots when we were kids. It was an economical vacation for us. Dad maintained that there's such an abundance of lakes nearby that it would be sinful to ignore them. We picked a different lake to explore each year. We would spend hours during the winter studying a map to decide where next year's vacation would be. Each of us was allowed to choose one holiday spot."

Maggie's lifted her wiener from the flames to inspect. It was plumped to splitting and evenly browned. Phil's bordered on burnt. "Just the way I like them," he observed as he buried it in a bun, topped with mustard and relish.

They had pulled the table closer to the fire to chase away the spring chill and the gusting wind. Instead, they endured the occasional cloud of smoke along with the heat. Overhead, an eagle screamed. They heard the splash as it plunged into the river in search of fish. The wind whistled through the trees, the fire crackled like milk being poured onto a bowl of rice krispies. In their protected secluded spot next to the fire, Maggie and Phil munched their hot dogs contentedly.

"Where did you pick?" Phil asked as he licked mustard off his fingers. "I mean, for a holiday."

Pushing her hair behind her ear, she smiled mischievously. "My choice was Waskesieu. It was great. There were all kinds of activities – hiking, tennis, the theater, shops, and arcades. Dad threatened to overrule my choice, but Mom came to my rescue. She said it wouldn't be fair. The year before, Jon's choice had been Candle Lake. So, Waskesieu it was – for the first and last time!"

"What was the objection to Waskesieu?"

"It's a resort town. Dad said that couldn't even be considered camping. There were lots of young people around. That was the real attraction for me. My friend Sylvia had been there, and she said every weekend carloads of guys would come from P.A. for beach parties." Maggie's eyes twinkled like sapphires in the sunlight. She hadn't thought about those days in a long while. "And Sylvia was right. It was the best summer."

Remembering the nightly bonfires, the water antics, the scantily clad guys and girls laughing, exploring their newly found freedom, brought a satisfying smile to Maggie's face. She had been more an observer than a participant, shy and embarrassed about her body for as long as she could remember. Nevertheless, that summer held a special memory – her first boyfriend and her first kiss.

The guy's name was Rodney Ecker. He had jet-black hair, worn straight back except for a wayward hank that insisted in falling over his left eye. His hair curled up at his collar, giving him the dangerous appearance of the teen idol James Dean. Heavy inky-black lashes shaded his ice blue eyes, and when he smiled, his crooked eyetooth was noticeable. Rodney was sixteen, two years older than Maggie. Recovering from a bad case of acne, he was as shy and inexperienced as she.

Rodney's father managed the Pool grain elevator in Spruce Home, an hour away, but he was staying with his aunt and uncle who owned a cottage at Waskesieu. His mother had died three years before while giving birth to her fourth child. His father found single parenthood overwhelming, especially with a newborn baby. He'd lost no time in remarrying – a widow whose husband had been killed in a logging accident. With her came her five-year-old son.

Rodney avoided his stepmother as much as possible, so when the opportunity arose to spend the summer working at Waskesieu, he jumped at it.

He worked at a boat rental place during the day, but most evenings were his own. Together they explored some of the hiking trails and more remote areas in the woods. They attended many of the beach parties, always just a little apart from the main group of teens. Neither one felt a part of the exuberant outgoing crowd.

It happened one evening during Maggie's last week of holidays. Rodney had come by later than usual that evening. They wandered toward the bandstand on the beach. A group called Smelling Rednecks from Saskatoon was playing. Maggie had brought an old gray army blanket to sit on. The small crowd slowly drifted away. Rodney was lying on his stomach propped up on his elbows, chewing on a stem of grass. "Wanna go?" he asked over his shoulder as the musicians packed up their instruments to leave.

Maggie was leaning against the trunk of a sturdy pine, watching the blazing ball that was the sun drop behind the black curtain of forest across the lake. Ignoring his question, Maggie spoke softly. "We're going home on Sunday."

Rodney sat up abruptly and tossed the grass away. He leaned back against the tree, his white T-shirt scraping the rough bark as he moved closer to her. Their shoulders nearly touching, he was close enough for her to feel his body heat. They sat that way for some time, looking out over the glassy water.

Then as if in slow motion, Rodney inched his arm around behind her head and rested it lightly on her shoulder. His fingertips gently brushed her arm. The tingling started where his fingers touched, rushing throughout her body. She turned to see if he was experiencing this electricity too. The slow motion, like a replay on TV, continued as he brought his mouth timidly to hers. It was as though a butterfly had landed on a rose petal. Maggie thought, 'This is just like in the movies!' They drew back to check the other's reaction. She laid her hand on his chest as he pulled her closer. They tried it again, and then, in a little while, again. Shyly, awkwardly, they explored. Urged on by raging hormones and boldness, their hands tentatively roamed over each other's arms, backs, necks, hair, and faces. Maggie could taste the grass he'd been chewing. The taste and touch of that first kiss was stamped into her memory.

To this day, whenever she saw a guy chewing on a blade of grass, Maggie remembered Rodney and silently thanked him for an unforgettable experience. It never failed to make her smile and wonder what ever happened to him. She never saw him again after that summer.

"It must have been some holiday," Phil said, interrupting her mental trip down memory lane. He noted how her face softened as the film played silently in her mind. Her eyes glowed with sentimental nostalgia.

Maggie brought her focus back to Phil, who was patiently waiting. "Sorry. It was a memorable time," she continued wistfully. "The next year Don chose Deschambault Lake. He's the serious fisherman in the family. It really sucked after Waskesieu, nothing to do but fish. We had fish for most of the following winter. How about you?"

"Our family was less adventurous. We always seemed to go to the same place – Little Bear Lake, because we had a cottage there. We would spend the entire summer there. Dad sold it five years ago, the summer after Mom died. Said it wasn't the same there without her."

Phil was poking at the dying embers with his wiener stick, coaxing a few more flames and sending up a cloud of ashes and smoke. Finally tossing the stick into the fire, he straightened up and brushed the ashes from his hands.

"Let's go for a walk. See if we can spot any geese," Phil suggested. He needed to shake off this melancholy mood. All this talk of family reminded him that he was now without a mother or a father.

They threw the remains of the picnic into the cooler and stowed it in the Jimmy.

The slides and swings were abandoned, the playground silent, as they headed down the sandy path to the lookout and swinging bridge. The Saskatoon berry bushes along the path were on the verge of bursting. Just a couple more warm sunny days and they would be cloaked in white blossoms and abuzz with bees. They walked in silence till reaching the lookout landing. It was built out over a point jutting into the river. Because the trees were still not fully draped with leaves, they could see in one direction past the marina toward the dam and in the other toward Eagle's Nest, the fishermen's landmark.

All was quiet below. The only sound was that of the rushing

water. Even the eagle had disappeared. They felt like the only two people on earth, held safely in the palm of Mother Nature's hand, watching the sunlight dance on the bobbing ice chunks and swirling eddies of the mighty Saskatchewan River.

A swinging bridge was strung across a deep gorge headed toward the river. Phil followed Maggie as she took a few cautious steps. In order to keep the bridge from swaying, it was necessary to co-ordinate their steps. Phil picked up Maggie's rhythm easily, keeping it fairly stable. The steel cables running along either side about four feet from the deck secured the steel mesh sides in place. They used the cables as a handrails. At the center, Maggie stopped and peered over the edge. The old waterwheel at the bottom was still mostly covered in ice and snow. A stream cut its way to the river. The trickle echoed off the sides of the dark ravine. They continued across the bridge to the water's edge.

Maggie wondered as they walked along the shoreline, their hands tucked into their pockets, why she felt so at ease with this man. Neither one had said much since leaving the fireside. The silence was not strained, but soothing, like her old well-worn comforter pulled around her on chilly winter evenings.

There were no geese, only the anxious river carrying the evidence of winter away. The road back up to the picnic area wound its way up the slope gently. Maggie desperately hoped Phil would not climb too fast or she would reach the top panting and out of breath, but he was content to walk at the pace Maggie set. She decided that she was going to set herself on a regular walking program. She knew Phil was involved in lots of physical activities. She wanted to be able to keep pace with Phil, should the need arise.

Phil was struck by the ease that had developed between himself and Maggie. Much as he loved Max and Jessie, he cherished this soothing silence.

When his niece and nephew had discovered him in the guestroom Friday morning, they barged in, jumped on the bed, kissed his face and tickled his feet until he came fully awake. Max and Jessie consumed every minute of his time since, playing games, drawing pictures or wrestling, leaving him hardly enough time to go to the bathroom.

Being here with Maggie was like going to a place of rejuvenation, an oasis. Even though she didn't fit his image of the perfect woman, he was strongly attracted to her. He found her easy to be with. He realized how strange this situation was – he liked Maggie and wanted to spend more time with her.

As she walked along beside him back up the hill, he admired her independence. If it had been either Sandra or Shelley, they would be complaining by now, whining, demanding his assistance in getting back up the hill. Maggie was definitely different. What would she feel like in his arms? As quickly as the thought popped into his mind, he erased it. Caution overruled. He didn't want to spoil things. 'Think with your head for once, not your pecker,' he commanded himself.

CHAPTER TEN

Easter Sunday church service was a showcase for the new spring fashions, like a sideshow at agribition – the annual agricultural exhibition that farmers from the area traveled to Regina to attend. The ladies in particular took note of the parade of oranges, brilliant yellows, quiet lavenders, and startling pinks. The sunlight illuminated the stained glass windows, casting subtle hues of blue, red and green over the congregation. Hilda Wilder worked her magic with the ancient organ. The welcoming strains invited regular churchgoers and visitors alike.

Phil, with Max clutching one hand and Jessie the other, followed Wayne and Joan to their usual pew, five rows from the back of the familiar church of his childhood. Max busied himself with trying to loosen the tie Joan insisted he wear, but to which he was unaccustomed. Jessie smoothed the full skirt of her new lemon-colored dress, opened her tiny white purse removing a Kleenex, a quarter, a pink hair barrette and a tube of lip-gloss. After the contents were all laid out beside her on the bench, she put them all back, slowly and precisely.

Phil watched the gathering crowd. It amazed him how many people were strangers to him. It was hard to believe that he'd been gone fifteen years. He was relieved to catch sight of Mr. and Mrs. DeLoone, who had lived across the street while he was growing up. And Mr. Kant, who had been the postmaster for as long as Phil could remember, still wearing the same cinnamon colored suit he wore to work every day of his life. He hardly recognized Delbert Stern, the class buffoon. He no longer looked like a court jester with wild and woolly hair. Now he was an ordinary bespeckled, slightly balding guy with a couple of pre-teen boys and a conservatively dressed wife trailing behind him.

Phil's attention was short-circuited by the entrance of the Mills family. Jackson led the troupe up the side aisle to an empty pew near the front. Lenore followed, then Don and Judy, Michael and Amanda, Maggie, with Jon bringing up the rear. His eyes were riveted to Maggie. Could this possibly be the same woman he shared hot dogs in the park with yesterday? She was stunning in a cobalt blue skirt and jacket, a milky white blouse with pearl buttons. Her auburn hair was held back with a gold clip. A fine gold chain was visible at the V of her neckline. Pearls adorned her ears. She was breathtaking.

He decided then and there that he was going to take her to a chic restaurant so he could see her all decked out again. He would be able to drink his eyes full and not have to strain to see around a dozen heads to get a peek at her. How could he think of a woman who looked like that as just a friend? Why had he never noticed her before? He'd been coming back here for years to visit family. Surely she'd been home for the same holidays, Christmas, Easter, Thanksgiving. It was like finally tripping over a gemstone that was underfoot all along.

Maggie was totally unaware of Phil and the rest of the Sanders family. Michael wanted to stay home and devour as many Easter candies as possible before his parents put a stop to it. The early morning Easter egg hunt had produced a huge basket of eggs and sweets to be sampled. Amanda behaved like royalty in her new Easter outfit, a lilac dress with white smocking across the bodice. Her outfit was complete with a white wide brimmed hat with ribbons part way down her back. She too had a snowy white shoulder purse.

Maggie wasn't sure who was squirming more, Michael or Jon. She leaned over and patted Jon's arm. "Be still," she threatened. "Or next time you'll have to sit beside Mom."

Jon winced, remembering long ago Sundays. He reached across Maggie, tugging at Michael's shirtsleeve. He motioned for him to sit between him and Maggie. As Michael settled in beside Jon, Maggie smiled, overhearing Jon's whispers. Michael got a run down of what could happen to them if their behavior didn't meet Lenore Mills' standard for proper church conduct. They both settled down and paid attention from that point on.

Reverend Adams took advantage of his captive audience. He

rarely had a packed church, only Christmas and Easter. Phil thought it would never end. After making his point for the third time since he began his sermon, he finally wished them all a Happy Easter and bid them a good holiday.

In the foyer and on the church steps folks visited, wishing each other a Happy Easter, shook hands with family members home for the holiday. Phil exchanged greetings with Delbert Stern. Delbert introduced his wife and children. He learned that Delbert had returned to town eight years ago and started his own water conditioning business. Phil listened somewhat impatiently, glancing over Delbert's shoulder into the church, waiting to get a glimpse of Maggie.

"Excuse me, Delbert. I see someone over there I want to say hi to. It's been great seeing you again." Phil clutched Delbert's hand in a hearty handshake. "It was nice to meet you, Bernice. Good luck with your business, Delbert."

Maggie emerged with Amanda by the hand. She raised her free hand to shield her eyes from the shock of sunlight, but not in time. She walked right into Phil.

"Oh, excuse me. I didn't see you." Recognizing it was Phil on whose solid chest her hand was resting, Maggie blushed and lowered her hand.

"Imagine not seeing a little guy like me," he joked, easing her embarrassment. He reluctantly removed his hands from her arms, where he'd caught her. This was a tangible woman, solid and real, not delicate and ethereal. The discovery registered in his face as bewilderment.

"I-I wanted to wish you a H-Happy Easter," he stammered.

"Happy Easter, Phil." Because Amanda was still clamped tightly to Maggie's hand, Maggie tugged her forward and introduced Amanda to Phil. "And this is my friend, Phil Sanders, Amanda."

Amanda politely shook hands, but her eyes surveyed this massive man from the top of his sandy-colored head to his polished shoes. Turning to Maggie with one hand propped on her hip, Amanda asked warily, "How come you never told us you had a friend named Phil, Aunt Maggie?"

Surprised by Amanda's frankness, Maggie replied hesitantly,

"Actually, Phil and I went to the same school and we met again at his dad's funeral a few weeks ago." She hoped this would satisfy Amanda. It seemed to. A moment later, Amanda spied her best friend Becky and dashed off to talk to her.

Relief spread over Maggie's face. She looked up to find Phil staring at her. "There's nothing like an eight-year-old's bluntness."

"That's okay. I've survived the inquiries of Max and Jessie about most aspects of my life."

Phil wanted to reach out and run his fingers gently along Maggie's ear to the pearl earring, to see if it felt like the satin it resembled. Instead, he commented awkwardly, "You look beautiful, just beautiful."

Maggie wondered if this nervousness was due to the fact that several folks had glanced their way watching the exchange, including both their families. Jon appeared to be waiting for Maggie so he could split for home and shuck his monkey suit, as he called it.

"Thank you, Phil. I'm riding with Jon and it looks like he's ready to go. Happy Easter, Phil."

Phil did not want her to leave yet. He was quite enjoying studying her. There were things he wanted to tell her, things he wanted to ask her.

"H-Happy Easter to you too, Maggie."

She turned to leave, walking toward Jon. He had to say something before she just walked away. Suddenly it burst out. "Wait, Maggie."

She stopped and turned to him.

"I had a great time yesterday. Could I give you a call sometime?" he asked anxiously.

What a dumb thing to say! He'd already said that once and then failed to follow through. How could she believe he was sincere?

A smile broke across Maggie's face. "Please do. Yesterday was the most fun I've had in ages. Thank you again."

Now relaxed and smiling, Phil returned firmly, "I will call this time."

CHAPTER ELEVEN

Spring – the days lengthened, the temperatures rose and the earth was adorned with greenery dotted with the blazing yellow of dandelions. In an agricultural community, it means some businesses experience their busiest season while others their slackest. Time crawled at Tobin Lake Motors as the farmers shifted into high gear, preparing the land and sowing the new crop.

Joan took holidays, so Maggie did double duty. Even that wasn't enough to keep her mind occupied at work. She cleaned out the filing cabinets, repotted the English ivy and the philodendron in the staff room, and polished the collection of model cars proudly displayed in the glass-enclosed case in the show room.

Maggie acted upon her resolution to become more fit. She checked out the programs offered at Simply Fit, the local gym and fitness center, signing up for an introductory yoga class on Wednesday evenings. She began a walking program, thirty minutes after work three times a week. She was surprised at how much she enjoyed the walking. It didn't seem like an effort. Each day she took a different route, enabling her to see neighborhoods she hadn't been through since she was a kid. She would arrive at home relaxed, the cares of the day left behind.

Maggie was beginning to doubt Phil's sincerity about calling after a week passed without a word. She tried to keep her mind from thinking about him. It was better that way. She wouldn't get hurt if she didn't care. It was okay for him to see her when it was easy and convenient but now that he was miles away, it would require too much effort on his part. Maggie was beginning to believe that if it didn't come easily, Phil wasn't interested. It was easier to rationalize his behavior if she believed him to be a smooth-talking cad that she did not need in her life. She was doing just fine on her own.

It was a Thursday during the second week after the Easter

vacation that Phil finally called, late in the evening. The ringing roused Maggie from the pages of LaVyrle Spencer's *Home Song*. Reluctantly she set the book on the ottoman and reached for the phone on the table beside her.

"Hello," Maggie yawned, glancing at the clock on the TV, wondering who could be calling at this hour, ten minutes past eleven.

"Hi, Maggie. It's Phil. Hope this isn't too late to call."

"Phil. No, it's okay. I was just reading and didn't realize what time it was." She sat up straighter in her chair, her senses suddenly alert.

"I bet you were thinking that I wasn't going to call again." He hoped she wouldn't just hang up but give him a chance to explain.

"To be honest, yes, the thought crossed my mind," she sighed.

"Sorry. Do you want to hear my excuse?" Phil asked, hoping to lighten the conversation.

He sounded so sincere. She was beginning to soften. "Sure, if it's the truth."

"Right, the truth," he sighed. "Well, here goes. When I got back after the break, Jason and his wife split. I told you about them, didn't I?"

"Your teacher friend?"

"Yeah. He's always helped me coach the track and field team, but this year he decided he couldn't spare the time, with his marital problems and all, so I was left with the entire program. I never realized until now how much he did in other years."

"Putting in some long hours, are you?"

"Hopefully the worst is over. The schedules are all worked out and I recruited another teacher to help out with the girls' team." He sounded exhausted.

Changing pace, he said, "Anyway, enough about what's happening here. How are things there?"

"It's been really slow at work with the farmers busy on the land. Joan took some holidays, but even with covering for her, the days have been crawling at a snail's pace."

"How are Florence and Harry doing?"

Maggie chuckled. "They have four babies and that keeps them both pretty busy. But just this morning while I was having breakfast

I could have sworn Florence was upset with Harry."

"What made you think so?"

She smiled, recalling this morning's drama. "Harry had just brought a fat earthworm and dropped it into a hungry mouth. Florence came to the edge of the nest and began squawking at him. It was really funny. I could just see this little lady with her hands on her hips giving him a stern sermon."

"How did Harry handle the situation?"

"He chirped a short apology and flew away."

"Smart guy." Phil paused, not certain about how to proceed. After a pause, he continued. "Like Harry, I too need to apologize. I wish I had called sooner. I feel better already just talking to you, Maggie."

"Apology accepted." She noticed how soothing his voice sounded, deep and slow. It had the effect of a gentle massage administered to tired tense muscles. Not wanting him to stop, Maggie added, "I like the sound of your voice, so please, continue."

Phil laughed, surprised by her bluntness. "That's a new one. I always thought my voice sounded like an echo in a tunnel."

"Hardly. You could be a hypnotist or a radio announcer if you chose. Your voice is very calming."

Maggie was definitely good for him. He could feel his mood lighten. He could hear her stifling a yawn on the other end of the line. "It's late, Maggie, but I wanted to know if you had plans for Saturday night."

"Nothing I can't change." Maggie had agreed to help her mom plant her flower boxes to fill the long hours of Saturday evening. It wouldn't be a problem to arrange to get the planting done in the afternoon.

"Great! Would you like to go for supper, some place nice and quiet?"

"Where did you have in mind? Here or there?" Maggie's surprise was evident.

"I was thinking there. I have boys' hurdles practice till 3:45 or so, but I could get there by six-thirty. How does that sound?"

"Good. I'll look forward to it."

"I'll see you then. And Maggie… thanks."

Maggie sat staring at the phone after she hung up. She was having a little trouble sorting out her feelings at the moment. Just about the time she decided Phil was a jerk and wouldn't call, he did. Furthermore, she had convinced herself that she really didn't care anyway. She didn't need the hassle. And now, he'd not only called but was willing to come to town to take her out. Maybe he wasn't the heel she made him out to be after all. He was sure doing a good job of keeping her off stride.

Better go slow, she cautioned herself. Phil had only asked her out for supper, nothing more. She couldn't afford to read too much into his invitation. He hadn't made an attempt to touch her since the night at her kitchen table when he took her hands in his. Maybe what he was looking for was a platonic relationship, a friend, and not a romantic involvement. He probably wouldn't even consider becoming intimate with a generous-sized woman.

The sound of his deep, low-pitched voice had stirred sensations low in her belly that she hadn't felt in a very long time. Blaming it on the lateness of the hour or maybe the mellow mood created by the novel she'd been reading, Maggie dismissed the sensation and began to seriously consider the possibility that she and Phil could be just friends.

CHAPTER TWELVE

Saturday finally arrived. The western skies were heavy with dark ominous clouds that threatened rain. Folks who were in the planting mode worked furiously, hoping to get the seeds into the ground before the rain fell. For those with sowing finished, a gentle rain was more than welcome. To those who had yet to finish, a rain would mean a delay. Everyone was concerned with the weather. In Saskatchewan the unpredictable weatherman determined futures and fortunes.

Maggie was anxious to get the window boxes and deck planters finished. She had lunch with her parents. Then Maggie and Lenore visited three greenhouses looking for just the right combination of bedding plants. Lenore knew exactly what she wanted – spikes, petunias, lobelia, and pansies in pinks and purples. They would be perfect against the white house with black trim. By four o'clock, the last purple striped petunia was planted just as the clouds released a gentle shower.

"What's your hurry, Maggie?" her mother asked, noting Maggie's agitation. "Wouldn't you like to come in for a glass of lemonade? I sure could use one." Lenore wiped her brow with the tail of the old checkered shirt she wore for gardening. She studied Maggie, waiting for a reply.

Maggie was trying to decide whether or not to tell her about Phil's invitation. Lenore knew her so well that she suspected something unusual was going on. Her mom had always been sensitive in that way. Sometimes it annoyed Maggie, because it seemed like her mom could read her mind. She could never have a secret for long. Finally she answered, "I can't stay, Mom. I'm going out tonight, so I want to go home and get cleaned up." She hoped it sounded casual. Maggie did not want her mom making a big deal of this, even though her stomach had been doing the jitterbug every time her thoughts strayed to Phil and tonight.

"Is it somebody we know, or shouldn't I ask?" Lenore asked cautiously, studying Maggie as she removed her gardening gloves, a smile playing at the corners of her mouth. She was plainly curious.

"Yes, you know him. Phil Sanders. We're just going out for supper. It's no big deal, okay." Maggie made an effort to sound firm.

"Okay, okay." It was obvious to Lenore that Maggie was touchy about the subject, so she would let it drop, for now, but she was obviously pleased. It had been a long time since Richard, and both Jackson and Lenore hoped Maggie would meet someone with whom to share her life. Maybe it was Phil Sanders. Lenore had always liked him, even as a bold and brassy teenager. Phil had a certain charm that was difficult to resist.

The doorbell rang just as Maggie was selecting a pair of earrings. The ringing chimes helped her decide. It would be the sterling silver native art ones with ruby-colored beads she had just picked up to try. She quickly fastened them behind her ears on her way to the door. She hoped that she hadn't overdressed. She had chosen a denim jumper with red appliquéd roses trimming the neckline and a red cotton shirt under it. She was surprised that it was a bit looser around her hips when she put it on, maybe due to the walking. That had the immediate effect of making her feel slightly more confident, even though her innards were still dancing a jig. It had been years since she'd had a date.

Phil was nearly as nervous as Maggie, even though his last date was only a few months ago. But this was Maggie, and he didn't want to mess up. She might not give him another chance. He buttoned, then unbuttoned the navy blazer.

Maggie thought he looked wonderful when she opened the door. He wore jeans and a blue pinstriped shirt, opened at the neck to reveal a few golden brown hairs.

"Hi, Maggie. You look great." He was amazed at how she always managed to look so coordinated, like she'd been put together by a professional designer. He wished he'd thought to bring her something. He felt awkward coming empty-handed. Next time.

"Please come in." Maggie stepped aside. As Phil stepped past her into the entry she picked up the scent of Colors cologne, one of Maggie's favorites. She liked it so well that she had given both her brothers a bottle last Christmas.

"Would you like a drink before we go?" Maggie asked.

"No, I don't think so. If you're ready, we can have one at the restaurant before we eat. Okay?"

"Sure. Just let me slip into a pair of sandals."

The Squire's Table was the most elegant dining spot in Nipawin. The pillars, posts and paneling were polished warm oak. The oak tables, graced with forest green colored linen tablecloths and creamy white tapered candles with ivy wound around the base set on brass holders suggested good taste. The wallpaper featured roses on a creamy background, the upholstery a deep rose color. The assorted live plants balanced the open atmosphere with hominess and privacy. Their table near the fireplace with a low burning fire invited coziness and conversation.

The aroma of hot Italian cuisine lured diners. Waitresses clad in black skirts and white shirts with black ties hurried about with heaping plates of steaming pasta, pizza or sizzling ribs. Garlic permeated their senses.

They ordered drinks, a beer for him and a Caesar for her. Their nervousness melted away like the candles. The relaxed comfort of their day at the park returned as they studied each other across the table.

Maggie liked the way Phil's hair didn't quite behave. It was thick and trimmed. He wore it precisely parted on the left, brushed to the side and back, but it refused to stay. It fell forward, covering part of his brow. It seemed to tempt her to lift it back in place, to restore orderliness. But those brown eyes gazing at her were still a mystery. The deeper she peered, the less she could fathom. Behind them, she sensed a man of conviction and purpose, a man who had spent time thinking about the wonders of the universe as much as why the Riders' last play in their final regular season game was intercepted. None of it showed on his face.

Phil was breathless, mesmerized. The candlelight reflected in the blue of Maggie's eyes, like moonlight shining on Little Bear Lake.

The shadows cast by the firelight created a mysterious aura about her. Her life was involved with much more than soap operas or the latest fashion trends.

She asked about his track program. He talked about a couple of guys on the team who showed the potential to advance to the provincial competitions.

He asked about her mom. She told him about her recent clear bill of health, her renewed interest in cleaning and gardening.

She asked about his friend Jason. He relayed how difficult it was to watch his friend go through such turmoil. It forced painful memories of his own loss to surface. He'd never really dealt with Sandra's death, only reacted to it by submerging himself in work.

"I think Jason and I have been grieving together," Phil said, finishing his salad. "Now, it feels like time to get on with life again. I mean really live instead of just coast along."

"That's kind of how I'm feeling about Mom too. I think she's going to be okay again, so I can direct my energy back to my own life. It has just fallen into place the past couple of weeks. When Lyle, at the dealership, offered me this position permanently, I wasn't sure what the right move was. I felt uneasy about leaving when it looked like Mom was just getting back on her feet, so, I decided to wait for a bit."

"Are you unhappy with your job?"

"Not especially. I just always thought that when Mom was better I would move back to the city. I sometimes miss the malls, the video stores. Stuff like that." Maggie was playing with her fork, thinking. "I guess, in a way, it's nice to walk down the street and have people know you, call you by name and ask how things are going. Now that I think about it, I really appreciated that while Mom was in therapy. It made me feel like people really cared. Maybe small town living isn't so bad after all."

The candles burned to stubs, the fire to embers. The lasagna they'd ordered was scrumptious and satisfying. The drinks, food and conversation erased all of Maggie's tension and jitters. She felt like Phil was someone she'd known and confided in regularly, someone with whom almost no subject was taboo.

Maggie's relaxed demeanor had a similar calming effect on Phil.

Concerns about screwing up vanished. Instead he relaxed and allowed himself to enjoy Maggie's company.

Outside the rain had eased to a light mist. The air was fresh with the smell of damp soil, emerging leaves and newly-washed streets.

"Would you like to go for a walk?" Maggie asked.

"It's still drizzling a bit."

"I know. I love to walk in the rain." Sensing his hesitation, she added, "If you want, we could stop and pick up an umbrella first. Or if you'd rather, we could do it another time."

Phil couldn't believe this, a woman who wanted to walk in the rain. It didn't seem to bother her that it would ruin her makeup and hair. Maybe she was testing him.

"Okay, if you're game, so am I."

Maggie ran into her apartment and grabbed a sweater while Phil found a parking spot down the street from Maggie's apartment building. He was waiting for her when she reappeared with the sweater flung over her shoulders and an umbrella in hand.

They headed in the direction of Chapman School; the elementary school they had both attended. It hadn't changed much, a couple of new swings and a climbing apparatus. Through the playground and into the Foxhole subdivision they continued.

"Do you ever think about having kids of you own?" Phil asked.

Startled by the question and not sure how much to share, she replied, "Sure, how about you? You seem to really enjoy Max and Jessie."

He stopped and stared at her intensely. "Of course, I want kids but I've had to accept that it might not happen." He wanted to add that he'd never met the woman that he would consider being the mother of his children – at least he didn't think so. But maybe he was looking at her now.

"Me, too. But I have Michael and Amanda." Maggie shivered slightly at the admission. She pulled her arms into the sleeves of the sweater.

Phil put his arm around her shoulder and impulsively pulled her against his side, giving her a firm squeeze. His warmth felt reassuring. Releasing her, he slid his hand down the inside of her arm until he found her hand and clasped it tightly. It seemed the most natural thing to do, walking hand-in-hand.

The contact sent currents skittering from her stomach. His nearness chased away the chill.

He stopped and dropped her hand when the familiarity of the street registered. They were standing in front of his childhood home.

"It hasn't changed much, has it?" Maggie asked, tucking her hands under her arms.

"Some. The trim used to be brown. I like this better." He inspected the new paint job. It sparkled white, the trim and new shutters the same green as the first leaves on the poplar trees. He could see that it had been reshingled, and the bathroom window had been replaced. The hedge was neatly trimmed, and crocuses proudly displayed their blooms along the front step.

"Who lives here now? Do you know?" he asked as he walked a bit further to see into the back yard.

Maggie followed him. "I have no idea."

"Hello, Phil," called a man's voice.

Turning to look across the street toward the source of the voice, they were surprised to see the DeLoones watching them from their porch swing. The honeysuckle bushes along the verandah nearly hid them from view.

Phil crossed the street in long easy strides. Maggie hurried to catch up. Phil rested his arms along the gate; happy to visit with his old neighbors again.

"Mr. DeLoone. Mrs. DeLoone. So nice to see you again. We were just admiring all the work somebody's been doing on the old place."

"Looks pretty good, doesn't it?"

"Do you know who lives there now?" Phil asked.

"A young couple with two kiddies. He's a conservation officer, and she works at one of the lawyer offices. Nice folks."

Finally Mrs. DeLoone could contain her curiosity no longer. Her eyesight was poor. The woman with Phil had said nothing. She couldn't tell who was out walking around the old neighborhood with Phil Sanders. "Who you got with you there, Phil?"

Phil reached for Maggie's hand and tugged her forward, his

dimples deepening as his smile broadened. His arm rested on her shoulder. "Sorry, Mrs. DeLoone. You remember Maggie Mills, don't you?

"Certainly, I do. How's your mom doing, Maggie?" Without waiting for a reply, she added, "She looked like her old self when I saw her in church Easter Sunday. A little thinner though, isn't she?"

"She's much better. Thank you for asking, Mrs. DeLoone." Here it was – the concern of hometown folks. Maggie smiled warmly, remembering Mrs. DeLoone's notorious nickname, "the newspaper." She could imagine that their walk through the old neighborhood would be the hottest news on coffee row tomorrow.

CHAPTER THIRTEEN

They arrived back at Maggie's place as the blackness of night crept over the town like a thick smog. The chill of spring had sent shivers through her body. As they left the DeLoones, Phil had firmly tucked Maggie's arm through his own, sharing their body heat. The heat of his big, smooth browned hand was welcome. It warmed not only her hand. The current spread from her fingertips, snaked along her arms, to the pit of her stomach and lower yet. She scarcely noticed the drizzle was soaking through her sweater and sandals. The umbrella hung from her arm, forgotten.

The warmth of Maggie's apartment welcomed them. Once inside, she lowered her head and shook like a puppy flinging droplets of rainwater on the walls, herself and Phil. When she lifted her head and saw through her disheveled hair the shocked expression on Phil's face, Maggie broke up. Laughter overcame her and she gave in to it. She threw her head back, clutched her sides and laughed from the depths of her belly.

"What's the matter? Never seen anybody do that before?" she chided him when she'd recovered momentarily.

"N-not for a very long time," Phil stammered, finding his voice.

"Go ahead and give it a try. It feels good," she challenged.

Phil eyed her suspiciously.

She placed her hands on her ample hips waiting, daring him.

A smile spread across his face.

"You chicken or what?" she taunted.

That was all the incentive he needed. He burst out laughing, bent forward, placed his hands on his knees and shook. In his best St. Bernard imitation, he sent water flying further than Maggie had.

When he opened his eyes, Maggie was sitting on the floor, legs spread straight out in front of her, her damp dress clinging to her thighs, hair disheveled, holding her sides in laughter. He slid down

67

the wall of the entry, collapsing on the floor across from her. With each glimpse of Phil's astonished face, Maggie burst forth with another gale of mirth. Finally, her laughter faded, his shock replaced by a relaxed awe. Neither moved as they scanned the other's face in the fading light.

Maggie was the first to break the spell. "If you'll excuse me a minute, I'll go get us a towel," she said as she reached down to flip off her sandals.

The light touch of his hand on her wrist stopped her. She lifted her eyes to meet his, soft and dark like the rich earth. With his other hand he reached over and carefully brushed the chestnut colored mop from her eyes. His fingers lingered, the tips slowly tracing the line from her cheekbone down to her jaw. "You're incredible," he said, his voice thick with emotion.

"Why, thank you," she replied softly.

He returned his hands to his lap.

"I am also slightly wet and so are you," she added. She rose and disappeared into the bathroom.

Maggie returned a few seconds later, her hair toweled dry and brushed. She tossed a downy soft, pink bath towel at Phil still sitting on the entry floor just as she'd left him. Then she headed for the bedroom.

When Maggie re-emerged in a navy blue sweatsuit with knitted blue woolen slippers on her feet, Phil was hanging his jacket on the back of a dining room chair. His loafers were neatly lined up beside her sandals on the mat near the door. The dampness had darkened his jeans at his thighs. He had hurriedly run a comb through the mass of sandy-colored hair. The part was slightly crooked. It was still damp, with that stubborn hank fallen rebelliously onto his forehead. The ruffled towel lay in a heap on the table.

Heading for the kitchen, she asked, "Could I interest you in a coffee or would you prefer something stronger?"

"What would you suggest?"

"Both, a shot of brandy and then the coffee." She already had the coffee started.

"Sounds good to me. Can I help?" he asked as he leaned against the end of the counter.

"The brandy and snifters are in there." She was pointing toward the door directly behind him. It was both pantry and extra storage space. "On the middle shelf to your left."

Maggie settled into one corner of the bulky forest green sofa, arranging the plump cushions to act as arm rests. Phil poured the brandy and handed Maggie a glass. Taking his own glass, he settled back into the opposite corner, tossing the unwanted cushions into the armchair. He raised his glass and leaned toward Maggie. She responded likewise. The glasses clinked. "Cheers," they said simultaneously. Each sipped the amber liquid while watching the other over the rim of the glass. This was new territory. A delicious tension was building, slowly and subtly.

Maggie broke the eye contact first, studying her glass, slowly swirling the contents. "I want to thank you for a lovely dinner. I don't remember when I last had such a good time."

"I especially liked the walk in the rain." A smile dimpling Phil's cheeks. "Even getting wet." The smile broadened. "Do you do that kind if thing often?"

"What? Walking in the rain?"

He nodded, taking another sip.

"I love to walk in the rain. This might sound pretty silly, but one of my fantasies is to get naked in the rain, some place private and secluded, lather myself up and let a warm rain rinse off the soap. Crazy, huh?"

Phil stared, making Maggie suddenly self-conscious, wishing she hadn't shared that fantasy.

"No," he answered thoughtfully. "It's just that you surprise me. I used to think I knew you, but I'm discovering that you are someone quite different than I had imagined."

"How so?"

"You're more spontaneous and fun than the girl I remember from way back when." The image of her frolicking naked in the rain played on the screen in his mind as he set his glass down. The idea of getting naked and crazy with this woman started his engines humming. But it would be best not to concentrate on such images if he was going to maintain any kind of proper behavior.

The gurgling of the coffee maker announced its readiness. While

Maggie got the coffee, Phil wandered over to the curio cabinet holding the bell collection. After noting some of the unusual ones, he shifted his attention to the tray of CDs beside the stereo. Flipping through her selection, he picked one and put it on. The calming, comforting melody of Mozart filled the room enveloping them like a feather quilt. The melody encouraged reflection and relaxation.

Both took up their positions on the sofa, first the brandy and now the coffee and music dissolving any reluctance as they melted into the cushions. Several minutes passed without any words spoken. Finally, Phil turned to study Maggie. Her head was leaned back, eyes closed, a slight smile pulling up the corners of her rosy mouth; her slippered feet propped up on the coffee table, swaying to the rhythm with her mug clutched in both hands resting on her abdomen.

"I've never really listened to classical music before," he admitted.

Almost against their will, Maggie eyelids cracked open, turning toward Phil. "Do you like it?"

"It's different. Why do you like it?"

"It seems to cover the entire gamut of human emotion. One moment it is calming and relaxing, then invigorating and animated, dramatic and passionate, then lilting and playful. It has the power to transport me through several planes of sensation in a few minutes. For me, it helps clear my mind, relax and begin again. It recharges me." She smiled broadly, just as the music shifted into a light up-tempo melody. His doubt was obvious in the slight crinkle on his brow.

"You need to get comfortable, clear your mind and let the music take you where it will," she explained, straightening up a little.

He listened, skeptical.

"Go on, lean back, put your feet up, get cozy." She took his mug and set it on the table. "Give it a try."

He slid down, wriggling his broad shoulders into the cushions, propped his stocking feet on the table, and closed his eyes, hands folded over his belt buckle. Maggie watched for several moments. She watched the lines on his brow dissolve, the hard line of his jaw relax, his nostrils become less flared, and even his cheeks looked softer. The rise and fall of his chest slowed, his breaths came more shallow. It was only when his head slumped to the side that Maggie realized he had fallen asleep. Smiling, she settled back into her corner, closing her eyes as Mozart began a dramatic concerto.

Phil was the first to awaken. Slowly he opened his eyes, at first wondering where he was. A smile creased his dimples when he looked about. Maggie was still stretched out in her corner, her head cushioned on the arm of the sofa, another cushion clutched to her stomach. The only sound was the rain gently splattering on the windowpane. He shifted softly so as not to awaken her, but enough to watch her sleeping face. Phil decided she looked perfect – content and relaxed, her dried curls falling across her glowing cheek, her generous rosy lips – teasing and tempting. He wondered how they would taste. He ached to touch, but, fearing he would startle her, he watched her sleep, giving his imagination license to fantasize.

Realizing the music had ceased and a knot gripped her shoulder, Maggie came awake slowly. When she opened one eye in a narrow slit, it was to see Phil watching her, smiling. She lowered her feet to the floor, leaned forward, reaching back to rub the offending shoulder.

"Have a nice nap?" he asked.

Glancing over her shoulder, she admitted, "This is a little embarrassing – falling asleep like this."

"Nothing to be embarrassed about. I was probably snoozing before you." Phil threw the cushions that were between them into the armchair and moved next to her. He motioned for her to get down on the floor in front of him. "Let me do that." He pushed the coffee table away with his foot.

Maggie checked to be sure that he was serious. He nodded affirmatively so she slid to the floor. She moved slightly forward to make room for him behind her. His big strong hands were surprisingly gentle. He gradually worked his fingertips along the cords across her shoulders and up the back of her neck. A sigh of relief escaped as Maggie lowered her head. "That feels wonderful. I think you've done this before." Her voice was muffled against her drawn up knees.

Her hair, though still damp at the base of her neck, slid through his hands like silk as he worked his fingers into the muscles along her shoulders and up her neck. "I coach track and football. Athletes get their share of muscle spasms and such. So I get to be coach, trainer, team doctor and masseur."

"Lucky for me." She could feel the hurt wash away, stroke by stroke, like the sand structures being washed away by the waves on the shores of Candle Lake when the wind rose. "How did you enjoy Mozart?" she murmured.

His hands slowed as he thought. "It must have a sedative effect, because I don't recall much of the music."

Maggie leaned back, her head cradled on the seat between Phil's knees and looked up at Phil, his hands resting on her shoulders. "Obviously. It took about three minutes to put you to sleep," she teased light-heartedly. "I lasted about fifteen."

As he watched her from above, slowly his hands moved to cup her chin and traced lightly along her jaw up to her ears. His thumbs lightly brushed her cheeks. His touch was so welcome. She closed her eyes to savor the sensations sweeping through her, from skin grazing skin. She was totally aware of this virile man and her own need. She could feel the firmness of his knees and legs against her arms. She realized that it had been a long time since she had allowed anyone to get this close. She yearned to know she was touchable, desirable. His caress was making her believe that she was all those things.

She felt his warm breath on her eyelids before she felt his lips light on her nose, gentle as a butterfly on a daisy. Then he planted an airy kiss on each cheek between his palms before reaching her lips. It was shocking, succinct and supple. The kiss sent tingling sensations through her limbs.

She reminded herself to proceed slowly. No need to hurry. This is a hormonal rush, nothing more. Hesitantly, Maggie twisted around until she was kneeling in front of Phil between his wide-spread thighs. With her hands resting gingerly on his rigid knees, she searched his toasty-brown eyes for sincerity. Ignoring her own advice, she whispered, "I've been wondering if you would ever kiss me."

"Does that mean it's okay?" he asked tentatively, covering her hands with his much larger ones.

He reached for her as she nodded. One hand sought the familiar heat of the nape of her neck, twining his fingers in her chestnut mane, while with the other he pulled her hard against his barrel chest. Maggie's arms encircled him. It felt like she was holding a warm, breathing, sturdy oak tree. She could feel his muscles tighten across his back, the warmth seep through the cool fabric as her hands glided over the cotton shirt. His lips, softly seeking, opened slightly. His tongue swept across her lips, inviting and enticing. She answered cautiously.

Her senses bolted to attention. He tasted of brandied coffee, smelled like a mixture of Colors cologne and rain. Pressed up against the denim of his jeans she could feel the oak tree stirring. Her racing heartbeat felt like a battering ram within her chest. The heat of his tongue seared her lips, her tongue. It flashed through her limbs, her body, to her toes, leaving her breathless, flushed and limp.

When they pulled apart, Phil took her face in his gigantic hands, balancing his brow on hers. He closed his eyes to stop his right one from twitching uncontrollably. A sigh seeped from his chest. "I've wanted to do that for some time. It's been driving me crazy wondering."

"Wondering about what?"

"Wondering what kissing you would be like." If the chemistry was right, he wanted to add. And how will this mess up my life?

She placed her palms on his tanned, smoothly shaved cheeks, then with one hand she nudged the hair on his forehead back up into place, only to watch it slide back down like a mud slide. "I've been wondering about some things myself." She smiled.

"Like?"

"Like – does your hair feel as good as it looks?" Like – can I trust those gorgeous brown eyes of yours?

"And the conclusion is…"

Combing it gently with her fingers and watching it fall back over his brow, she answered, "It feels like velvet, rich and luxurious."

With his arms linked around her, he drew her closer. She definitely was more of an armful than he was used to, but it felt strangely comforting, solid and secure, holding her like this. There was no mistaking the urges coursing through his groin. He looked into her sapphire blue eyes, and there was no doubt Maggie Mills was a sensual and sexy woman. He knew he had to get out of there soon before he was tempted to do something totally dishonorable! Just one more taste. He lowered his head, his mouth to hers, exploring, probing, seeking.

She quivered as he slid his tongue lightly along the edge of her teeth. The touch of his hands caressing her spine was firm and reassuring. Her hands brushed his wayward hair. She let her fingers fondle his ears and trail down his neck into the collar of his shirt.

Suddenly, he caught her lower lip between his teeth, nipping it gently. She could feel a smile travel across his face. As she brought her hands to rest on his cheeks again, she could feel the dents in them.

"Time to go," he said as much to remind himself as to inform Maggie. Just one more kiss.

He lifted his jacket off the chair and slipped into it. He glanced at the clock boldly displaying lateness – twelve forty-five. "I'd better be going." Turning to face her, he set his wrists on her shoulders, his fingers playing with her hair. "I should have no trouble staying awake on the drive home after that little snooze."

Gingerly she placed both palms against his chest. "Thank you for the best evening I've had in ages." When he chuckled, she added, "I'm serious, Phil."

Covering her hands with his and clutching them against his chest, he observed, "It's the first time I've taken a woman out, walked in the rain, flailed water like a retriever just out of the lake and fallen asleep listening to Mozart. This has been a memorable evening. I'll call you soon."

He surrounded her with his arms, hers slipping inside his jacket around his middle. They stood clinging to each other for several minutes, rocking slightly, stamping the impression of the other's body on their memory. He pushed her hair from the side of her neck and nuzzled his face into the curve of her neck, drawing a deep breath to imprint her fragrance. The urge to snuggle up to her for several more hours was tempting, but reason prevailed.

Drawing back, they studied each other. "It was terrific. I'll talk to you soon," he whispered.

Neither moved. Finally, he bent and branded her one more time with a lingering, luscious, and lusty kiss before bolting out the door.

CHAPTER FOURTEEN

Days later, Maggie was still buoyed by the electricity of her Saturday evening with Phil. After he'd left, she lay awake till well past three-thirty, reliving the new direction their relationship had taken. She had forgotten how a kiss could make her heart hammer and her stomach shimmy. She shuddered, remembering his hands spread wide across her shoulder blades and up the nape of her neck. She hadn't felt this vibrant and alive in a long time. She walked through the days as though in a protective bubble of joy, nothing could dispel her delight with life. She kept her reservations at bay. Her heart prevailed over her head.

Phil's gut felt like he'd been on a Ferris wheel for one ride too many. Each school day ended with a headache, the result of intense concentration to keep his mind on classes and track practice instead of daydreaming about Maggie. His evenings were spent puzzling over this bizarre situation. He'd been married before, twice, in fact, but he'd never experienced anything like this. With Sandra, he felt certain she was what he wanted, so he went after her single-mindedly. The ride was short, intense, unplanned and ended like slamming into a brick wall at sixty miles per hour, leaving him barely alive. With Shelley, it was like catching an Amtrak train speeding in the wrong direction and getting off at the first stop after the mistake was realized. But with Maggie, it was totally different.

The arguments raged on into the night. He prided himself on being seen with beautiful women, and Maggie wasn't gorgeous. But she had those breathtaking, big, sky blue eyes! He liked the stares he got when he escorted minuscule women like Sandra and Shelley. Maggie was not tiny. In stocking feet his chin rested on the top of her head and he would describe her as rotund. In his arms she felt like a precious gem, a diamond compared to a zircon, yet soft and sensual. Perfect! Oh, to hold her like that again!

It was such a nuisance that she was in Nipawin and he in Prince Albert. They couldn't just spontaneously go for coffee or a walk or a movie. But wasn't last Saturday worth the effort? He'd had a great time.

Maggie was thirty-six by his calculations, and he was turning thirty-three next week. Maybe she still thought of him as the jerk he was in high school. Would she take him seriously? Three, four years difference was nothing at all. It didn't seem to bother her the other night. She seemed serious enough when they were kissing. And how she could kiss! Made all the blood rush from his head to his groin.

And what about children? Maybe she thought she was too old to start a family. She'd said that she was resigned to never having children of her own, her niece and nephew were enough. Well, not for Phil. He took for granted that someday he would have a family, just as soon as he met the right woman.

And on and on the arguments raged till the early morning hours. He wished he could just pick her up and go for a hamburger or watch a pee wee baseball practice or go hiking in Little Red River Park. They needed to talk. He did the next best thing. He called. And he called often, usually late.

Maggie's was the voice he heard last before sleep. Sometimes it was brief, just the opportunity to hear the other speak, sigh or yawn, while other times they discussed and dissected various topics, from Canada's role in the war on terrorism to teen suicide to the ramifications of insufficient funding in schools.

Phil shared his concerns about being able to build a lasting relationship. He felt jinxed. He'd struck out twice already.

Maggie spoke of her life-long task of coming to terms with her body. How some days she felt confident and complete, and how on others she wished for a shape considered beautiful by society's standards.

But Phil's most pressing concern went unvoiced. The time never seemed right. He knew that Maggie had thrown his comfortable routine into chaos.

Phil was attempting to concentrate on preparing his senior students for their upcoming track meet just prior to the long weekend in May. More practices were scheduled as the event grew closer.

Some evenings he arrived home late, hungry, tired and aching. The ache was not entirely physical, he realized as he flopped on the couch, staring at the TV, dining on a can of beans with soda crackers and a glass of milk. What did he have in his life that really counted? His routine? Living alone, coming home to an empty apartment? Was he willing to settle for so little because he was in a rut? He yearned for the security of a home and family, someone to come home to, someone to share his frustrations and triumphs with, someone to ease the ache in his soul, like Maggie.

He checked the time. Ten forty-five. Dusting the cracker crumbs from his T-shirt, he reached for the phone just as it rang. It was Maggie.

"Hi, I thought I would surprise you for a change."

"And a pleasant surprise it is. I was just about to call you." He paused. "Gee, Maggie, it's good to hear from you."

"Had a rough day?"

He slouched back into the cushions, his muscles relaxing, and her voice acting like a liniment soothing the aches and pains. "Not especially. I'm not sure I can describe this... just a weird, lonely, achy feeling."

"Are you coming down with something?" she asked, concerned.

"No, I don't think so. Just keep talking and I'm sure I'll feel better." He could hear her chuckle. "Seriously, Maggie. I always feel better after talking to you."

"I know what you mean. I feel the same way. I love to listen to you talk."

"Maybe that's why we have this long distance telephone relationship."

"Maybe. Actually, that's why I was calling. I was wondering if you were tied up with practice every night?" She charged forward before he could answer and she lost her nerve. "I just read in the paper today that the drama club here at the high school is presenting *Fiddler On The Roof* this week. I thought if you were free and interested, I would try to get tickets." Out of breath, her fingers crossed, she added, "What do you think?

Suddenly a wave of panic overtook her. She swallowed it down hard and wondered if she hadn't lost her mind. She really didn't need Phil complicating her life, but it was too late now. She found herself acting against her better judgement.

He sat up, picked up his day planner and flipped the pages forward to check his schedule.

It felt like forever to Maggie before he answered. Maybe he was searching for a way to decline without hurting her feelings. Maggie could hear the pages rustling.

Finally, he mumbled, "Yeah, I could rearrange a few things and make it Friday. How does that suit you?"

"Sounds great," she sighed with relief.

"I'm afraid that I have to be back here for Saturday though. I have agreed to work with two of my senior boys perfecting their high jump technique. Both have natural ability but a shortage of practice time because of part-time jobs. From noon to three on Saturday is the only time they can both make it for practice."

So it was agreed that Maggie would pick up the tickets tomorrow.

Before hanging up, Maggie said, "I hope you're feeling better, Phil."

"Was I not feeling terrific?" he joked. "I feel wonderfully sleepy. Thanks, Maggie. I needed a boost," he answered lightly.

"That's what friends are for. Goodnight, Phil."

Maggie realized that Phil was becoming a trusted friend. She spoke with him more often than she did with Eileen now. They could discuss many topics with ease. It was like they were on the same wavelength at times. Phil viewed most issues in terms of black and white, right and wrong, while Maggie saw more gray areas. When she questioned his position or he hers, hours whizzed by – while their phone bills climbed.

Friday couldn't come soon enough to suit Maggie. She picked up the tickets the next day. Phil called that night to confirm. He sounded as excited as she was.

Maggie stopped to have coffee with her mom and dad on Thursday evening. She'd been out walking, to burn off excess energy, which was pumping through her. She couldn't concentrate on anything, so the solution was to walk. Her mind could race off in any direction, totally independent of her feet. The subject of her mental forays was primarily Phil Sanders.

One glance at Maggie and Lenore knew something was brewing, but she would have to wait for Maggie to talk. Lenore knew how Maggie loathed being questioned – cross-examined, Maggie called it. So she would have to wait till she was ready to spill the beans. But maybe a bit of prodding wouldn't hurt.

"Maggie, what a surprise! You just out walking?" Lenore asked as casually as possible.

Dropping into a kitchen chair, she replied, "Yeah, I've been out nearly every evening since the weather warmed up." ·

"You look great. What's new?"

"Nothing," she answered defensively.

The conversation shifted to safe topics, the brilliant pink and purple flower beds and pots, Jon's latest phone call to Lenore and Jackson the evening before, when the missing lights at the only controlled intersection in town would be fixed and the previous nights baseball scores.

Finally Jackson, having little patience with the games his wife played with Maggie, asked directly, "Are you seeing that Sanders boy?"

Taken by surprise, Maggie studied her father's worried face, then could barely suppress a giggle. "That Sanders boy, Dad, is no boy. He's thirty-two or thirty-three years old. Have you seen this boy lately?" she asked, emphasizing the word "boy." Reaching across the table, she patted his roughened hand. She made a mental note to check his birth date.

Jackson Mills was not a man of tremendous stature, the years of hard work had taken their toll, but he would make a formidable opponent if his family was threatened. Against Phil, he would look like a bantam rooster pitted against a turkey gobbler.

"You don't have to defend my honor, Pop. I can take care of myself." Planting her hands firmly on her abundant hips, she snickered, "I'm a big girl. See!"

"You still haven't answered my question, young lady," he continued unwavering. He was not about to relax until his mind was set at ease. He'd heard on coffee row about Maggie and that Sanders boy out strutting around town in the rain a couple of weeks ago.

Now he wanted to know what was going on. He didn't want to see Maggie hurt again. He remembered all too well how despondent she was after Richard deserted her.

Maggie was a private person. She intended to keep her relationship with Phil as low-key as possible until she knew if it would evolve past friendship. Her attempts at not thinking too far into the future were not always successful.

Images of a relationship beyond friendship with this brown eyed, dimpled man troubled her. They were unforeseen, unbidden, and often unspeakably outrageous. Maggie was not ready to admit that this budding relationship with Phil was forcing her to rethink her life plan – that of remaining contentedly unattached to avoid any further pain.

Looking across the table into her father's troubled grey eyes, Maggie could see the anxiety in the grooves marking her father's brow.

"Dad, we're friends," she said at last. "We're getting to know each other, that's all." She squeezed his hand. "Okay? Relax, please."

"So you have been seeing him," her mother stated after she watched her husband wheedle the facts out of their daughter.

She'd heard about the walk in the rain before Jackson came home with the news. Mrs. DeLoone had called the next day to inquire about Lenore's health. During the conversation she just happened to mention that she'd seen Maggie the previous evening, out strolling with Phil Sanders. It had reminded her that she should call Lenore. Only incidentally did she ask if Maggie was seeing Phil, and wasn't Phil Sanders married?

"We went out for supper one time. Remember, the day I helped you with the planters? That's all."

"But I thought you didn't like him. You said he was an arrogant flirt. Remember? I was the one who always liked him," Lenore reminded her.

"That's what I thought when we were in high school, but that was a long time ago. We've both changed since then." Maggie wanted them to believe this was a casual acquaintance, nothing more.

Lenore persisted. "So, you do like him then?"

"Yes, I like him, and this will be enough interrogation for one evening. Okay?" Maggie was becoming flustered. They meant no harm, but sometimes they still treated her like she was nine years old, especially when they feared she might be hurt.

Lenore poured Maggie more coffee. She wasn't about to let the subject drop without a parting comment. She added smugly, "Maybe the thing you've been searching for all your life has been right here in your hometown all along. Right under your nose, and you just never noticed."

CHAPTER FIFTEEN

The lights dimmed. A hush fell over the audience as the orchestra struck the first notes of the opening. The auditorium of the high school had been transformed into a theater. The entire town had been buzzing about this production for weeks. The cast included several local adult would-be actors and actresses, a few elementary school children, as well as Mick Stang's drama students. Mick called upon the technical resources within the community to lend a hand to his crew of high school whizzes.

The skeptics whispered that Mick had bitten off too much with this undertaking, but he was one to challenge the limits of himself and his students. He believed this was going to be their best production yet.

The show had opened two nights earlier. Maggie had spoken to three different customers about it while they waited for their cars to be serviced. They had attended and were still raving about the superb job done by actors, musicians and support people alike. They said it was as good as any performance one might see at the Touchstone Theatre in Saskatoon. Maggie was looking forward to the evening.

Maggie and Phil arrived just five minutes before the curtain went up. Phil was glad he'd met no police patrolling the highway on his way to Nipawin. He broke the speed limit in order to pick up Maggie and get to the school on time. He sighed and settled back into his seat, relaxing. He reached over and picked up Maggie's hand, squeezed it firmly, leaned toward her, and whispered in her ear, "This was a wonderful idea." He brushed his lips across her cheek as he straightened up again. A smile spread across her face as she whispered back her thanks.

Reverend Miles Layton of the Presbyterian Church played the lead role of the Jewish Russian peasant Tevye, while Adele Bracert, the high school music teacher, played his wife. Both were superb.

Tevye's rendition of "If I Was A Rich Man" brought thunderous applause.

Maggie was very aware of the stares they'd received when they entered and found their seats. Let them look, she thought. Mr. and Mrs. DeLoone, sitting three rows in front of them, waved coyly when they were getting settled into their seats.

It had been a rush for her to be ready when Phil arrived. She had been delayed at work until nearly six o'clock, finishing the night deposit for Joan, who was called to school at coffee time. The teacher called to say Max was sick and could Joan come and pick him up. As a result, Maggie finished her day's work and then Joan's as well. She rushed home, showered, changed clothes, fixed and ate a tuna sandwich before Phil arrived at seven-fifteen. She sank into her seat and allowed the music and drama that was unfolding on stage to transport her to another time and place.

During intermission they wandered out into the hallway and toward the pop machine located by the school cafeteria for a cold drink. "What do you think? Are you enjoying it?" Maggie asked.

"It's excellent. I had no idea there were such gifted actors in this town. Do you know this Miles Layton? Has he been in town long?"

"I asked Joan that. She said he arrived about two years ago. I have never seen him before, but he sure can play the part. And that voice!"

Sipping his Pepsi, Phil agreed. He was watching Mick Stang scurry from the stage to the dressing rooms to the sound stage and back again. "He's still like a cat on a hot tin roof," Phil observed.

"I didn't know you knew Mick. He didn't go to school here, did he?"

"No. I got to know him in university. We were in several classes together, mostly English. He had a natural bent for drama even then." Phil laughed, remembering a scene from those days. "I'm not sure he would appreciate the stories I could tell. He joined the university's theater company, the Saskatchewan Players. During our freshman year, they did *Romeo and Juliet*. Mick argued with the director throughout rehearsals because he wanted to rewrite the ending. He said the one Shakespeare had written was stupid."

"Stupid?"

"Yeah, he couldn't see any good reason to die for love. He insisted that any normal guy would just get over it and find another woman. Simple as that."

"The simplicity and naiveté of youth." They enjoyed a hearty chuckle at Mick's expense.

Phil followed Maggie back to their seats for the second half of the performance after they had finished their drinks. Phil checked out the orchestra as they reassembled. He recognized a couple of members. Luther Wilks, the whiz in Mr. Donald's biology class, now managing a local seed processing plant, was playing the clarinet. In the back row playing the violin was Mr. Toller. He retired some years ago after selling his successful insurance business to Sal Purts. Phil wondered how Mick had assembled such a diversified troupe. The conductor, a young, darkhaired lad who looked more like a mechanic than a musician, brought the chatting to an abrupt halt when he raised his hands to begin the scene's opening number as the lights dimmed.

Maggie was fascinated by the performances of the young girls who played Tevye's daughters. A Broadway production couldn't have been more sincere. They looked like they were born to be on stage, something Maggie envied. She found it difficult enough just trying to be Maggie, never mind learning to become another character.

She glanced over to find Phil totally absorbed in the action on stage. He seemed to particularly enjoy the performance of the matchmaker. He had a difficult time stifling his mirth whenever she was on stage. And then, all too soon, it was over. The appreciative audience rewarded the players with a long and noisy ovation.

Phil tucked his program into his jacket pocket. "Do you mind if I say hello to Mick if I get a chance to see him?"

"Certainly not. He has done a terrific job. He's to be congratulated."

Half an hour later, they were walking through the balmy May night air to Phil's Jimmy. They'd had to park three blocks from the school. Maggie looked up at the sparkling ceiling overhead and drew a deep breath of the night air. It reminded her of the smell of just washed bedding hung on a clothesline to dry. "This is perfect." The sky seemed blacker and the stars more brilliant without the glow of the street lights.

Phil pulled her to his side and left his arm resting on her shoulder.

A gentle sexual stirring swept through her. She felt secure and serene. At this moment, all was right in her world.

"I am glad you suggested this, Maggie. I never would have thought I'd run into Mick Stang again. Especially here, tonight. He looks like he's enjoying himself. Was he proud or what? It's a wonder he hasn't popped the buttons off his shirt." Phil chuckled.

"And so he should be."

"And those kids! Boy, what talent."

Two hours later, they were contentedly stretched out on Maggie's living room floor facing each other, propped up on fat floor cushions while David Foster played "Man In Motion" on the stereo. The empty pizza box lay on the floor between them, inside it four empty beer cans. Maggie provided the beer. Phil had suggested the pizza. He was famished. Before leaving home, he'd emptied the contents of his fridge, that being two wrinkled carrots and an apple.

When they'd arrived at her apartment with the pizza, Maggie had spread a red checkered tablecloth in the middle of the floor while Phil fiddled with the stereo. When he turned around, Maggie was seated cross-legged, pouring beer into a mug, the pizza in the center sending aromatic waves throughout the room. She handed him the frosty mug and poured another for herself. "I hope you don't mind camping out like this."

With a goofy grin pasted on his face, Phil made himself comfortable opposite Maggie. "My first indoor picnic this year." He drank deeply. "Thank you, this tastes delicious."

"Don't tell me that you've never had a picnic indoors?" Maggie eyed him suspiciously.

"Not in recent memory," he admitted.

Now, David Foster played on as Phil studied Maggie in the soft glow of the lamplight. The gleam illuminated subtle golden streaks in her silky chestnut hair. The blue of her eyes darkened several shades to Prussian blue in the shadows. They beckoned.

She watched the light soften the brown of his eyes and play with his devilish dimples. She ached to move closer, to finger those dimples, kiss his sumptuous mouth, nuzzle her nose into the curve of his shoulder and breathe deeply.

As though he could read her mind, he inched closer on his elbows till they were nose to nose. His lips found hers, gently at first, testing, tasting, then more urgently.

She responded as his tongue slid over her upper lip. A jolt rocketed through her, igniting her desire.

He tasted slightly yeasty from the beer. His fingers were in her hair, sifting, combing the silkiness. He pushed her back onto the cushions, shifting his attention from her mouth to her jawline, teasing her earlobes, nipping, tracing the tip of his tongue along the edges.

The shivers scattered through her limbs.

He felt her tremble. Then he returned to her mouth. Their breaths had become rapid and ragged.

Maggie wanted nothing more than to wallow in this plane of thoughtless pleasure, to ignore the warning bells tinkling in the recesses of her consciousness. How far are you prepared to go, Maggie? What happens if he wants more than a few searing kisses and fondling? Will he head for the door faster than greased lightning if he sees what you look like under your clothes, bulges, rolls and all? How will you handle the humiliation if he does?

Finally, Phil rested his forehead on her chin, taking a deep breath and filled his senses with her fragrance. She smelled so wonderfully woodsy and all naturally woman. He wished there was a way to wrap her essence about him, to act as a buffer. With her he could relax and just be Phil, no pretenses. He did not feel a duty to protect and pamper her as he had felt obliged to do in previous relationships.

She felt more like a partner, like together they could challenge the world, face any storm. He knew Maggie Mills was the strongest woman he'd ever met, and she intrigued him.

But still, he wondered. I'm not getting any younger and if she doesn't want a family, maybe I'm just wasting precious time here. If I'm going to turn my life upside down, I need to know it's for a relationship that has some promise.

Maggie had never questioned this aspect of this new relationship before. She steadfastly refused to entertain the possibilities, dragging her mind back to reality. She believed that allowing herself to dwell on the future was to cast a curse over it. It was better to take it a step at a time. It was her protection against hurt.

Now, here she was, flat on her back in the middle of her living room floor with Phil splayed across her breasts, kissing and fondling. She found it profoundly arousing.

She sensed his hesitation as he did hers. With her palms on his cheeks she gently raised his face to look into his eyes. There was passion and pain swirling in the brown depths. "What is it?" she whispered.

A sigh escaped as he leaned over and kissed her lightly, then sat up. Combing his hair back off his forehead with his fingers, he choked, "My timing is really lousy, but much as I'm enjoying this, I think we should talk." He gazed down at her, imploring her to understand.

This must be serious, Maggie thought. This went against all her preconceived notions about men, Phil in particular – that he would choose talking over a sexual romp. She sat up, yoga style, rearranged the cushions behind her, and planted her elbows on her widespread knees. "Do you often change directions in midstream like this?" she teased, trying to lighten his seriousness.

He shook his lowered head.

Reassuringly, she reached over and squeezed his hand. "Okay. Let's talk."

"I'm not sure how to put this. I've been meaning to bring it up before now, but the time was never right somehow. Not that this is the right time either." He was struggling, staring at the floor.

She stopped him with a hand on his arm. "Phil, remember when I told you the one thing I expect is honesty? Whatever it is, say it. I thought we'd become good enough friends that no topic was off limits."

"Okay." He raised his troubled eyes to study her reaction. "Do you want to have kids?" he blurted out. Without waiting for her reply, he added, "You said you were prepared to settle for a niece and nephew, that they were enough. I need to know because I'm not getting any younger." Anguish clouded his expression. "I'll be thirty-three next Thursday."

A sober Maggie thought for a few minutes about how to best express her feelings before she replied. "Of course, I wanted children, but after Richard left, I didn't think that was an option any longer." She took a deep breath to center herself before proceeding. "So I decided it would hurt less if I made up my mind to appreciate my brother's children and give up the idea of ever having my own."

So there could be no misunderstanding, she added, "I imagine you are also aware that I'm older than you. I'll be thirty-seven in August."

"What does that mean? That you can't or would choose not to have kids now?" As an afterthought, he added," And, yes, I know how old you are."

Maggie considered her response carefully. "It means that time is running out." Maggie watched the realization flicker across Phil's face. "Yes, I could still have children. But to change my mind at this point would mean that I was involved in a stable relationship, one where children would be wanted, loved and supported. I believe that children should enhance an already good relationship, not be a substitute for one." She felt passionately about that. If this relationship was to ever amount to anything, he needed to know that she believed having children was a monumental decision, not a reckless consequence.

He watched her face become earnest as she shared her views. He was relieved by her answer. Children were an important issue to both of them. At that moment, watching her face change from playful to solemn, Phil was struck dumb. He was in love with Maggie Mills.

CHAPTER SIXTEEN

The fragrance of rain-washed vegetation assaulted Maggie's early morning brain when she cranked open her kitchen window. She halted momentarily, inhaling deeply. Absolutely nothing smelled better than the morning after a May shower. The earth was alive, showing off its splendor. Brilliant colors were splashed about like a carefree artist gone mad with inspiration.

Maggie's next thought was of Phil. Today was his birthday and she was still undecided about a gift for him. She didn't want to give something too personal, and yet it had to be special. The dilemma had robbed her of a good night's sleep.

The ringing telephone interrupted her musings.

"Good morning, Maggie," her father's voice greeted her. "I hope I didn't wake you."

"Morning, Pop. I was just admiring this gorgeous morning. What's up?" She could hear the excitement in his voice.

"Your mother and I were wondering if you had plans for the weekend. This is the long weekend coming up, isn't it?"

"It sure is. As for my plans, I picked up a stack of books from the library that I'm dying to dive into. Other than that, nothing. Why?" She was suddenly wide-awake and itching with curiosity.

"We thought it might be fun to hook onto the camper and spend the weekend fishing at Little Bear Lake. If you'd like to come, you could read there. What do you think?"

Within minutes, it was decided that Jackson and Lenore would leave as soon as they were ready, to ensure a family campsite. Her parents had spoken to her brothers the previous evening. Don and Judy would bring their camper after work on Friday. Jon had agreed to bring his tent with the understanding that Michael would share it.

Maggie didn't have to think long about her decision. It had been years since she'd been to Little Bear. She knew her mother must be feeling like her old self again to have suggested this family gathering. Maggie was looking forward to it. But it didn't solve her immediate problem – Phil's birthday gift.

Or maybe it did. A couple phone calls later and it was arranged. Maggie was as pleased with herself as she was with all God's creatures today.

Maggie's walk to work was brisk, a skip in her step and anticipation in her heart. The robins were bathing and cavorting in the puddles before the sun could suck them up. Maggie's entire world had a freshly cleaned and polished sheen. This was going to be a great day.

And it was. But by eight o'clock that evening, Maggie was pacing. Her bags were sitting on the bed, already packed, needing only the last minute items. She'd dug out her hiking boots and set them by the door.

Why hadn't she heard from him yet? She was sure the phone would be ringing off the hook when she came in from work, but not a word yet. He probably had practice after school again. Tomorrow was the field meet. That was hardly an excuse. Maybe he hadn't liked her gift. Well, so be it, Maggie decided as she marched off to the shower. She wasn't going to waste her time waiting for him to call.

At ten-thirty, the long awaited call came. Maggie had just made a cup of tea and was studying the word search puzzle in the paper.

"Hey, Maggie. Thanks a million. This has been one terrific birthday. You won't believe what happened today!" he babbled excitedly.

"Well, tell me about it," she said with a chill in her voice. "It sounds like you are still revved." A smile curled her lips as she felt the excitement in his voice. She began to thaw a bit.

"At ten minutes to noon, I was just handing out assignments to my English class when we heard this noise in the hallway. It kinda sounded like tiny Christmas bells tinkling but not really. The entire class went dead silent. Finally I went to the door, and there stood this ancient little man. He was dressed in khakis and a red checkered flannel shirt and high top rubber boots." Phil stopped for a second to catch his breath, having missed the coolness in Maggie's voice. "But listen to this, Maggie, that's not the best part. He had fishhooks and weights and bobs and lures and leaders and every fishing apparatus or gadget you can imagine tied or pinned to his clothing. He marched right into the room with all those contraptions clinking away, removed his battered old fishing hat, held a fish net over his heart and belted out 'Happy Birthday.' You should have been there, Maggie. It was really something. Then he approached me, tucked an envelope into my pocket and wished me a 'Good Day' as he was leaving. The kids just sat there mesmerized. Nobody said a word. After I dismissed the class, I went to the staff room and opened the envelope. I was just dying to find out who would do such a thing. I could hardly believe it was from you. And a gift certificate from The Fishing Hole. What a great idea! Thanks a million, Maggie," he finished in a flurry.

"You're welcome, Phil. I do wish I'd been there to see the expression on your face. Now, tell me, what took you so long to call?"

"Within an hour of the singing fisherman's' appearance, everyone in school knew it was my birthday. The news spread quickly. The secretary ordered a cake for after school, and then there was practice. Jason had left a message at the school office. You remember me telling you about Jason, the guy who's separated. Well, he called to say he was taking me out for supper. When we got to the restaurant, there were half a dozen other friends waiting to surprise me. I got home ten minutes ago. I could hardly wait to call you. And that's the real story. Honest!" he added with emphasis.

"Okay, okay. I was just dying of curiosity." Relieved, she sat back and propped her bare feet up on the opposite chair. "I'm glad you've had a memorable birthday."

"The only thing that could have made it better, would have been if you could have been here to share it. I thought about that at supper. How I wished you'd been there, Maggie," he said softly.

"I wish it too." And she did. "When are you going to pick out your new fishing equipment? I sure hope you need some."

"You bet I do. I've been drooling over the new sports catalogues all spring. I was thinking maybe I'd go have a look Saturday."

"Good. Buy something special."

"By the way, what are you doing this weekend? I almost forgot it was a long weekend with this track meet tomorrow. I've been pretty focused on that."

"Actually, I have plans. I just finished packing. The entire family is going camping at Little Bear. Pop wants to go fishing. What has us more excited is that Mom suggested this. She hasn't felt up to something like this in a long time. What about you? Doing anything special?" she asked casually. Maggie had hoped to see him on the weekend, but since he hadn't mentioned anything she saw no reason to let her disappointment ruin the first long weekend of summer.

"I haven't given it a thought yet. I guess I'll be going shopping for some new fishing equipment though," he laughed. "If I need to try it out, I guess I know where to find the Mills family fishermen, don't I?"

The very idea gave Maggie's heart a quick kick to start it racing. "Sure do. Mom and Dad left today to get a camp spot for all of us."

"Would anybody mind if I just popped in?" This was a plan worth considering, Phil thought. He hadn't been to Little Bear in a long time.

"I doubt any of my family would object."

"How about you? Would you mind?" he asked cautiously.

"I most certainly wouldn't mind. I would love to see you again."

"When are you going?"

"I'll leave right after work tomorrow."

"Maybe I'll see you on the weekend then."

Maggie sure hoped so, even if it meant bringing the stack of books she'd borrowed from the library back without having turned a page.

CHAPTER SEVENTEEN

Amanda squealed, dancing on one foot as the frog she was tormenting leaped onto the toe of her sneaker. Maggie howled with laughter, watching the spectacle. The two had been on a nature walk for the past hour. Maggie cherished this time with her niece. They had spotted several species of birds – swallows, robins, wrens. They had stumbled across a ducks' nest containing five precious eggs near the water's edge and spied a doe with her fawn grazing in a meadow near the landfill. Crouching in the tall grass, they observed the deer unaware for several minutes before Amanda grew fidgety. The dash for cover was immediate when the doe's alarm system sounded at the crackle of a twig.

Both Amanda and Michael awoke at dawn. Grumbling and groaning followed soon after. Nobody else was as anxious to vacate the cozy confines of their beds as the two young early birds.

Maggie had been the first to arrive Friday evening, in time for a late supper with her parents. Don and Judy rolled in well after dark with two sleepy bundles, Amanda and Michael, in the back seat. Jon arrived an hour later. By the time they were all set up for the night, it was midnight.

Jackson built a fire. The aroma of campfire coffee drew appreciative sighs. The adults settled around the fire, relaxing with coffee and cookies before retiring.

The blackened evening sky glittered with dancing stars above the treetops, like rhinestones strewn across black velvet. It appeared close enough to run one's fingers over the dark, cool sleekness. The exhibition overhead grabbed their attention. Quiet filled with calm reverence settled over the Mills family gathered around the fire. The sleepy bunch found their respective bedrolls soon thereafter. Maggie shared the camper with her parents.

"Do some people really eat frogs, Auntie?" Amanda asked as

94

they continued along the trail back to the campsite.

"Yes, they are considered quite a delicacy by some people," Maggie replied, wondering where this line of questioning was going. She thought the frog incident was long forgotten when Amanda had spotted a ladybug clinging to her shirtsleeve.

"What do they taste like? Have you ever eaten frogs?"

"No, I haven't. But a friend of mine tasted them – they only eat the legs. She said they tasted a little like chicken. Why do you ask?"

Carefully cupping the ladybug in her palms, Amanda stopped walking and turned to her aunt. "We talked about this in kindergarten last week. Mrs. Rogers, that's my teacher's name. She said that if you were lost in the forest you could eat stuff you find, so you wouldn't starve. I was just thinking I would have to get really, really, really hungry to eat a frog." Her face was screwed up to convey her distaste.

"Me, too, Amanda. Does this mean you're getting hungry?"

Nodding her head vigorously, she replied, "Very, very hungry!"

"Then lets get back to camp and see if we can rustle up some lunch."

By the time Maggie and Amanda arrived, the fishermen had just returned with their morning catch, eight walleyes, commonly called pickerel by local fishermen. Don and Jackson volunteered to fillet the fish while Jon and Michael built a fire. Michael and Amanda were ecstatic when Jon, having consulted his mother, announced that hot-dogs were on the menu for lunch.

Near four o'clock, Jackson awoke from his snooze in a reclining lawn chair. The fire from earlier was reduced to coals – just perfect for marshmallows, he decided. Stirring up the embers, he called to Michael, "What do you say, we have a snack before we see if there are any pickerel left in that lake?"

Michael came running, the squirrels he was feeding quickly forgotten. "Right on, Grandpa. Maybe I'll get the biggest fish this time."

Jackson disappeared into the camper and reemerged with a giant bag of marshmallows. "That one you caught this morning was no baby fish, Michael. It was almost as big as mine."

The slender willow branches that had been sharpened for the wieners were reused again for roasting the marshmallows. It didn't take long before the entire gang was engaged in the serious business of roasting marshmallows, teasing and laughing. Michael's mouth was outlined with marshmallow. Amanda's fingers were stuck together. Jon had just poked a perfectly toasted, plumped marshmallow toward Maggie's face. He popped it into her mouth before purposely dropping a dollop of the soft gooey center on her nose. Hilarity abounded.

This is how Phil found the Mills family when he arrived. He stepped out of his Jimmy and for the first time since he'd had the inspiration to surprise Maggie, Phil had a doubt about whether this was such a wonderful idea. Seeing them all together like this, laughing and playing, Phil felt like an intruder. His twitching eye conveyed his apprehension.

Maggie came to his rescue. She hoped her delight at his appearance wasn't discernible on her face. Even though she was delighted to see Phil, she did a quick visual survey of her family's faces. She saw surprise on all the faces, except on her mom and dad's. Pleasure was registered on theirs. She came out of her lawn chair to greet him, swiping at the marshmallow on her nose. "Phil, what a surprise!"

"I just got some new fishing equipment I'm itching to try out," he announced.

When she'd nearly reached him, he lowered his voice, leaned over and whispered. "You look delicious topped off with marshmallow. Would it embarrass you if I just licked it off, right here and now?" He chuckled, watching the color rising to her cheeks and the red blotches appear on her neck. He had a sudden urge to wrap his arms around her and kiss her soundly.

Softly, she answered, "Yes, so behave yourself." Then, for all to hear, she said, "I think you are just in time. Dad said he was going out again. He would probably let you tag along." Turning toward the rest, she asked, "What do you think, Dad? Do you think you can show this guy how it's done?"

Rising to the challenge, Jackson stretched to he feet and extended a hand to Phil. "Good to see you again, Phil. We'd be pleased to take you out with us, wouldn't we, guys?"

Watching the exchange, Michael finally piped up. "Who's this guy anyway?"

Feeling quite superior, Amanda answered with her arms folded across her chest, "He's Auntie's boyfriend, stupid!" Laughter broke out everywhere as greetings were exchanged.

Amanda decided she wanted to try her hand at catching a fish. Don warned her that there was no toilet on the boat, so she had better go one more time before leaving. Lenore, Judy and Maggie went down to the dock to see Amanda off on her first fishing experience with the rest of the crew.

Maggie watched Phil as he eased himself into the boat beside Jon. He arranged his brand new tackle box under his seat. He looked marvelous, an old battered Blue Jays ball cap pulled low over his eyes, the sun glinting off his cheeks giving his face the glow of polished copper. He was wider across the shoulders than Jon, although they were about the same height. Lenore gave the same instructions she'd always given for as long as Maggie could remember, "You catch 'em, we'll cook 'em." With Jackson piloting the trusty craft, they sped off to their favorite pickerel hole.

Maggie was poking around in the coals of the dying fire to find the foil-wrapped potatoes she and her mother had placed there earlier when Phil crouched beside her, brushing against her arm. She could feel the radiated heat. The contact sent shivers up her arm. The look in his eyes sent the shivers snaking throughout her body.

He'd been wanting to get his hands on her since he'd arrived. The fishing distracted him for a time, but once they were back on land, his thoughts ventured to when and where he could get her to himself. He could hardly keep himself from reaching for her, like a parched man restraining himself so as not to let it be known how badly he needs water.

"Here." He handed her a beer. "You look like you could use this." She wasn't sure if it was the heat from the fire or the one he'd started within her that had her perspiring.

"Let me help," he offered. She took the beer gratefully and

handed him the tongs. "How many more are in here?"

"Three." She watched the muscles in his arm flex as he extracted one more. Despite the noise of everyone chattering, Maggie lowered her voice. "I really am happy to see you, Phil. I was kind of hoping you would decide to come here… to try your new equipment, of course!"

"Of course." He shifted his attention from the task at hand to her face. Her cheeks glowed with warmth, her blue eyes lively with teasing. "Maybe we could go for a walk later… alone," he emphasized.

Supper was freshly caught pickerel, pan-fried to perfection as only Lenore could do. Jon helped Judy prepare a salad while Don and Michael laid out the table. Two picnic tables were set end to end to create a long dining table. Nearby, Jackson was demonstrating for Amanda the art of casting, using a discarded willow roasting stick as a rod, to which a weight was secured with a string.

"This is the best fish I've ever tasted," Phil remarked with enthusiasm, polishing off the last piece.

"I agree. You haven't lost your touch yet, Mom." Don praised Lenore's efforts. "Looks like we've eaten today's catch. We'll have to go out again tomorrow. What do you think, Michael? Amanda?"

"Now that Grandpa showed me how to cast, maybe tomorrow I can throw my own line in the water, Dad. You won't have to do it for me anymore," Amanda announced proudly. "Will you come too, Auntie?" she asked. When Maggie hesitated, Amanda continued convincingly, "Fishing is fun. Really it is. You'll like it."

"I know, Amanda. I've been fishing lots of times."

"Then will you come?"

"Maybe I will. I'll think about it till tomorrow."

Not satisfied yet, Amanda tried another approach. She turned her attention to Phil. "Could you please talk to her, Phil?"

Surprised at the request, Phil stuttered, "S-Sure, I'll try."

After dark, the night sounds echoed through the campgrounds. Children's voices were quieted except for a baby crying somewhere. A couple of dogs could be heard in the distance. Shania Twain's "Don't Be Stupid" blasted from two campsites down. On the lake a

98

boat was coming in to dock.

The Mills campsite was quietly contented. Jackson had challenged Jon to a game of checkers. Don was settling Michael into Jon's tent, while Judy tucked Amanda into bed in their camper. Lenore was enjoying a cup of coffee by the fire. Maggie reached for Phil's hand. "Let's go for a walk." He'd been waiting hours for the invitation.

They walked hand in hand, neither saying anything till they were well past the string of campsites along the shoreline. Then he stopped in the middle of the road and gathered her into his arms. "I've waited all day for this." His voice was husky with wanting. His mouth found hers. There was an urgency in his embrace as he flattened her breasts against his massive chest. The kiss was passionate and rough as his teeth raked across her lips. The murmur in her throat was her only reply. Her fingers sifted through his hair, then her arms tightened around his neck. They might have remained entwined indefinitely but for the glare of the headlights of an approaching vehicle.

Phil grabbed her hand and pulled her to the side of the road. The tension of the moment broken, they started laughing. "This could be dangerous," he joked.

"That's just what I told myself on more than one occasion, starting with your dad's funeral."

They continued on toward the water, her hand still snugly fitted into his.

"What, me… dangerous?" He sounded surprised.

"I knew it would be dangerous for me to get mixed up with you the minute you peered through me with those brown eyes of yours," she confided. "I felt like you could see right into my soul."

"Truly? I'm far from dangerous," he denied. Her revelation was unexpected, in addition to being unbelievable. He… a simple man… dangerous. "I want to know you, Maggie… your dreams and desires, your ideas and insecurities, your fears and frustrations." Playfulness had switched to profound. "I would never knowingly hurt you." He studied her face in the darkness for understanding and confirmation. "Believe me!"

They'd arrived at the beach where benches were tucked in under the protective boughs of the massive spruce trees. They sat facing the water, watching the crescent of a moon shimmer across the water in streaks. The loons' eerie, heartbreaking call sounded from further down the lake. They sat in easy silence for a time. Phil's arm rested along the back of the bench, his hand gently massaging Maggie's shoulder. Her right hand rested on his thigh where he stroked it with his own. The need to touch was paramount.

Maggie dropped her head back against Phil's arm. She turned to him. "This feels so good. I have missed you."

"I know. I feel the same. I was thinking on the drive here that it's only been a couple weeks since we went to Mick's drama night, but it feels like two months."

"I've been keeping busy, but even that doesn't help much," Maggie confided.

"God, I know. My rationale is that by the time I drop into bed at night, I'll have to sleep because I'm totally exhausted. But as soon as my head hits the pillow, it's like my mind switches to another channel – the Maggie channel."

She chuckled quietly. "The Maggie channel? That's good, Phil."

"Don't laugh. It's true, and it's not funny. Exciting, erotic, but definitely not funny"

Maggie reached over and stroked his cheek tenderly. In the darkness she couldn't see him clearly, but she could feel him and smell him. Her hand went around into his hair. Gently she drew his face to hers. The meeting was less urgent this time, yet sweetly passionate. One kiss turned into two, then two into many.

Somewhere in the back of her consciousness, a small voice warned her of the heartache she vowed she'd never go through again. Consciously, she turned off that voice to concentrate on this moment and the pleasures it held.

She needed to savor Phil, banking the tastes, sensations and aromas for future lonely nights. Maggie's head swam, her body tingled.

Phil felt the shiver. Breaking contact with her lips, he whispered, "You cold?"

"Uh-uh," came the reply. "I just can't get enough. You have the most fascinating mouth."

"Oh, really." He traced her lips with the tip of his tongue. "Be my guest. Help yourself."

She did just that. Their tongues danced a provocative tune, dipping and delving.

His body stood at attention until his loins ached with a need for her. Slowly he brought his hand from her back forward, stopping at the side of her breast. Gingerly his thumb reached out circling. He felt her moan more than heard it. He sensed that she too wanted more. When his hand was filled, he marveled at the generosity of her. His thumb found her nipple through her sweater. He massaged it timidly till it stood erect, straining for freedom. He knew only that he ached to touch and taste all of her. His imagination tormented his senses.

Maggie knew the moment he reached to touch her breast with tender hesitation that she had fallen in love with this big burly bear of a man. He respected her sensitivity about her body size with casual ease. The realization lasted only a moment. Then, an insight flashed through her mind – this was the man she'd been waiting for all of her life. She'd better consider this carefully.

The enlightenment sobered her. She broke away, gasping for air. She reached for his hands and held them between her own, searching in the reflected moonlight to read his face. She discerned confusion and lust. "We had better stop now before we can't," she whispered.

"I want you, Maggie. That's pretty obvious. I also want to be with you, to know all of you. When I'm not with you, I'm miserable. When I am with you, I ache for more, and that makes me miserable, too. Funny, isn't it?" Reflected in the moonlight, his face wore the misery he described.

"No, it's not funny. I feel the same way. I believe it's either love or madness, Phil." She planted hard, passionate kisses all over his stunned face. "It's okay, Phil. I think I love you," she said quietly, allowing the news to sink in.

"Are you certain? This isn't just some new way to torture me?" Phil could hardly believe what Maggie was saying. He'd hoped this might happen with Maggie, but he had reservations because of his history of failed relationships. She was everything he wanted in a woman – kind, funny, smart, honest, generous, loving and the best friend he'd ever had. Could this be for real?

Maggie wrapped her arms around his neck, nuzzled his chin with her nose, kissing the line up to his earlobe and then back to his mouth. "Yes, I love you, Phil Sanders," she said, listening carefully to the sound of the words said aloud. "Does this feel like torture?" she asked playfully.

He groaned, "Yes, but delicious torture it is." He held her tightly. "I can hardly believe that you really do love me. A guy who has failed twice at marriage. You're sure?"

"Positive!"

"I love you too, Maggie." Cautiously, reverently, he kissed her anew as though he'd just crossed the boundary into sacred territory.

Her hands slid up beneath his sweatshirt, exploring the cushion over his ribs, the quivering muscles of his back, the edge of his jeans around to his waist. Lightly she reached up to feel the silky curls from his waist expand upward and spread across his hard chest. He was holding her gingerly. He sucked in her breath with his when her fingers fanned his nipples, teasing, arousing.

Her hands rested there as his glided up under her own sweater. Her insecurity reared its ugly head. This was where he would stop, repulsed by the enormity of her, when he actually had his hands full of her flesh. She was sure of it. She heard him moan, his long thick fingers seeking more, caressing.

"I want to feel all of you. I want to make love to you," he said huskily against her mouth. He found the clasp on her bra. It gave way. His palms came round to acquaint themselves with her fullness. Carefully he explored without the restrictions of clothes. Her nipples stood upright, and his thumbs registered their texture and reaction to his stroking.

Maggie's tension faded with his apparent appreciation of her body. She was grateful for the darkness. A river of heat raced from her nipples to her core. Her legs went numb. The calls of the loons, traffic noise, the close proximity of other people faded from awareness, the sensations she was experiencing demanded her total attention.

Phil tore his lips from the warmth of her neck. "Much as I would like to ravage your body right here and now, I don't want our first time to be an uncomfortable, hurried coupling on a bench at a public beach. I love you so much. You deserve better than this, Maggie." He watched her regain control of her emotions, her lips trembling. "I want it to be right," he vowed firmly. "As soon as we can arrange it, okay?"

She wouldn't argue. This wasn't where or how she had imagined it would happen either. It needed to be special. Hesitant to abandon her exploration of his torso, she asked, "How about my place next weekend?"

"It can't come soon enough to suit me. How will we possibly get through the rest of this weekend?" he asked, trailing kisses down her cheek, gently squeezing her breasts.

"In agony."

CHAPTER EIGHTEEN

Despite the fact that the holiday made for a shortened workweek, time crawled like a plump, lazy caterpillar in the hot summer sun. Maggie anticipated the coming weekend. Her concentration was often broken by images of Phil, naked in her bed. She blushed at the thought like a nervous virgin. She was euphoric. She could hardly believe how her entire life had changed when they acknowledged their feelings for each other. Her resolve for a spinster's life had vanished.

They had snatched only a few minutes alone throughout the rest of the weekend at the lake. Maggie spent the nights in her parents' camper while Phil unrolled his sleeping bag in the tent with Jon and Michael. Both lay awake long after everyone else. They listened to the loons call across the lake and allowed their imaginations the freedom to soar since they'd made the decision to take the next step in their relationship. A logical step and one they could hardly resist much longer.

Phil remembered the fullness of Maggie's breasts, the softness and warmth.

Maggie yearned to feel the tremor of his chest muscles beneath her exploring fingers.

Business at Tobin Lake Motors had picked up. The buying public was shopping for the best deal in town. Maggie and Joan were swamped with telephone and in-person inquiries. Maggie preferred the interaction with people to the clerical duties her job involved. Her days were packed with both.

Maggie had taken some time off on Wednesday afternoon to see Dr. Staeger for her routine medical check-up. Not good timing. The office at work was buzzing when she left. Joan would do the best she could till Maggie returned. Next year she would arrange this appointment during the spring sowing season when business was slow anyway.

The waiting room was overflowing with an assortment of patients, from runny-nosed children to incapacitated old-timers. Impatiently, she waited for her turn.

In her cubicle she stripped out of her clothes and waited Dr. Staeger's arrival draped in a thin piece of white paper. It annoyed her that the sheet barely covered her breasts and abdomen. Surely every woman undergoing this routine pelvic examination was not the size of an overgrown mosquito. That was about all the sheet would modestly cover.

Maggie had chosen Dr. Patricia Staeger because she was her mother's doctor. She respected Staeger's concern and thoroughness when Lenore had discovered a lump in her breast. She'd outlined Lenore's options and her own recommendations with compassion. That seemed good enough for Maggie.

Dr. Staeger bounced into the room with her usual vitality. Her cocoa brown eyes and hair were the crowning highlights in an angular face and willowy, thin body. Cute described her better than pretty. Maggie sometimes wondered where she got her seemingly endless supply of energy. She seemed to manage her medical practice and family of three children with energy to spare. She looked nothing like any doctor Maggie had ever seen, in a banana yellow jumpsuit and sandals. She looked like she just stepped out of the beauty parlor rather than surgery.

"I thought I would get it out of the way while things were slow at work, but it seems I've miscalculated."

"Busy, is it? Well, this won't take long. The nurse has already taken blood and urine samples, hasn't she?" Maggie nodded.

"Any problems I should know about?"

"No. I feel great. I'm doing this to please my mom more than anything. She's been nagging me about having a check-up."

"It is time, Maggie. Your last complete was over two years ago according to the information you supplied." Dr. Staeger was doing her best to look stern. "But I understand about mothers. Mine is always on my case about eating properly," she grinned. "Mothers will always be mothers no matter how old they get."

The Pap smear finished, Dr. Staeger removed her gloves. The breast examination was next. "I haven't seen your mom in a while, Maggie. It must be time for her to come in again for a check-up, too. Tell her I said that."

Dr. Staeger's fingers moved expertly over Maggie's right breast, then her left. In the area closest to her underarm, Dr. Staeger pressed and prodded with extra attention. "Have you noticed this before, Maggie?" She placed Maggie's hand over the precise spot. "Feel that?"

Maggie applied pressure, and through the soft tissues she too felt a nub of rigidity the size of a marble but not as hard. "No, I never noticed that before." She felt the fear instantly creep up her throat, threatening to choke off her breath. It left a metallic taste in her mouth, like biting on tin foil.

"It may be nothing, Maggie, so don't worry. Have you ever had a mammogram before?"

Maggie shook her head, too stunned to speak, her mind whirling with disbelief.

"I do think you need to have a mammogram just to make sure it's nothing serious. With your mother having just been through a bout with breast cancer, you can't be too careful, Maggie. I'll go see when we can schedule one while you get dressed. Then we'll have a talk."

Maggie dressed in robot fashion; her mind reliving the emotional turmoil she'd experienced while her mother was being treated. CANCER – what horrible images it evoked for her! The very word belonged in the same category as terminal, mutilation, agony and loss.

Later, Dr. Staeger returned with the forms. "We have you booked for a mammogram in Prince Albert in two weeks." Dr. Staeger pulled up a stool and sat facing Maggie, close enough to rest a hand on her arm. "There's no point in worrying about it yet, Maggie. Eight of every ten growths we discover are benign. Chances are excellent that yours will turn out to be non-cancerous as well." Dr. Staeger peered into Maggie's eyes for some sign that what she was saying was registering.

Suddenly Maggie realized the importance of the information Dr.

Staeger was giving her. It could save her life. She tried to focus on the doctor.

Dr. Staeger explained about the mammogram, how it was done and why it was vital in detecting cancerous growths. She also told her how to prepare herself for the examination – no deodorant, powders or creams. She suggested wearing a two-piece outfit for ease of undressing.

Maggie's mind swam with a million questions; Did it hurt? How long did it take? When would they know the results? Then what would happen?

"I am going to give you some literature to read. If you have any questions or concerns after that, call me, Maggie. After the procedure is over, it takes a few days for them to get the results to us. Come back and see me a week or so after, and we'll discuss the results. Okay?"

Maggie nodded dumbly.

Maggie walked back to work, hardly noticing where her feet were taking her. This is stupid. You cannot afford to let your imagination go crazy like this. Just because Mom had cancer, doesn't mean that you do. You are a healthy woman. You can lick this. Now pull yourself together. You have a job to do. And Maggie did – just barely enough to get through the rest of the day at work.

Later that evening, Maggie decided to take a drive out to the park. She needed to clear her head of the jumble of thoughts and do some constructive thinking. She parked near the playground where several children were scrambling up and down the climbing apparatus. She strode along the edge of the playground till she reached a hiking trail. A few more steps and she was alone. Nature provided the model of serenity she badly needed.

The chatter of a chipping sparrow perched on a branch at eye level broke through her thought barrier. She stopped momentarily to notice. The sparrow tilted its head when she asked quietly, "And what might your crisis be today?" The bird flew away at the sound of her voice.

Maggie continued down the trail till she came to a tiny stream babbling over rocks on its way to the river. A fallen spruce tree provided a perfect seat. She removed her sneakers and socks to dangle her feet in the icy water.

What about Phil? She loved him, but would this change their relationship? Should she tell him about the lump? Maybe he'd want to cancel their weekend rendezvous. Maybe he'd come out of pity. Was she obligated to tell him? Would it change how he saw her? Maybe he could tolerate her body, as it was now, overweight but healthy. He might be totally revolted by the idea that she had a lump that could be cancerous.

How would this change her own self-image? How could she feel like a complete woman if they removed her breast? How could Phil possibly love her if they mutilated her body?

Should she tell her parents? Her mother would worry herself sick. And her dad, how would he deal with another cancer threat in his family?

What about the family she'd begun to hope might be a possibility with Phil? Could she still have children? Was it fair to Phil to begin a sexual relationship under these circumstances?

Maggie was suddenly aware that daylight had faded to dusk. She slipped her socks and shoes back onto her numbed feet. The walk back was brisk and invigorating. The park was deserted by the time she returned to her car. Back home she sank into a hot bath and soaked while a Strauss waltz echoed through the rooms of her apartment.

By ten-thirty, physically and mentally weary, Maggie crawled into bed. Her confusion drained away with the bath water. She'd decided that she would do as Dr. Staeger advised. She would not worry about possible outcomes until the results were in. She would wait.

Even though she loved Phil, and he loved her, they had made no commitment to each other. There was no point in complicating their situation, she reasoned. There was no point in causing him to worry, especially if it turned out to be nothing. She also decided not to tell her parents. There was no point in subjecting them to that mental anguish when it might be nothing serious. She'd spare them all the anxiety for now.

Phil called just before she nodded off. He apologized when he realized she was sleeping.

"No problem, Phil. It's good to hear your voice." The truth was his low sexy timbre sent tremors down her spine in anticipation. "Just keep talking."

"Are you okay, Maggie?" Phil recognized the weariness in her voice.

"It was a tedious day. I had a long hot bath that made me sleepy, so I just snuggled down here a few minutes ago." She sat up, plumping her pillows up behind her. "How are you doing?"

"Don't laugh, but this feels like the longest week in history. Will Friday ever get here?" His voice was quiet, low and pleading.

"I know exactly what you mean. It's the same for me. Joan asked me what happened on the weekend that had me so absent-minded this week. Apparently she said something to me a couple times that I didn't hear. A dead giveaway according to her."

"Did you confess?"

That brought a chuckle from Maggie. "No. I told her it was quite an interesting fishing excursion and left her to ponder the meaning of that. Have you told anyone about us yet?"

"No, but when my brother Wayne called on my birthday, he wondered what was bringing me to Nipawin so often, since I hadn't stopped by their place the last time I was there. He heard I was in town for Mick's drama production. That's his way of letting me know that he knows about us."

"Mom and Dad interrogated me one evening. It seems Mrs. DeLoone called Mom, to see how she was doing. She just happened to mention that she'd seen us out walking and was wondering what was going on."

"How did you reply?"

"Honestly. I said we were getting to know each other, becoming friends."

"True. In a few days we can say friends and lovers. I like the sound of that. Till Friday, Maggie Love."

CHAPTER NINETEEN

He had called her Maggie Love on the phone the other night. He had never used any form of endearment before. She liked how it sounded when he said it, so unexpectedly. It reminded her of something a rugged Scotsman might say to his beloved wife of many years. It amazed her that it could cause her heart to skip every time she thought about it.

Maggie smoothed the creases from the rough white linen tablecloth with care. She wanted every detail to be perfect. She arranged the plates, wineglasses, and silverware. A bright bunch of daffodils in the center of the table sang praises to Maggie's impeccable planning. Brilliant yellow linen napkins resting beside the plates were twisted in knots, like Maggie's stomach.

Maggie wasn't sure when she'd last been this nervous. She'd showered and dressed with care in a navy and white sundress. She chose her best underwear, hoping it wasn't too suggestive. She wondered how and when she'd take them off. Or perhaps Phil would. The thought raised goosebumps along her arms. Would it be slow and deliberate, after a leisurely evening with supper and wine, or would it be frantic and immediate?

Maggie had promised herself this one indulgence before she faced the consequences of the lump in her breast, just one weekend of loving while her body was still intact. She had taken her robust health for granted until now.

Her self-consciousness about her plumpness became secondary. Phil had not been unduly concerned about or turned off by her size to this point. He had assured her that he loved and wanted her as she was. If he was repulsed once her clothes were removed, then that would be his problem, she decided. She would have more threatening ones to deal with soon. But, despite her intentions, she wondered about his reaction.

Phil had promised to stop for Chinese food on his way out of town. Maggie picked up a bottle of wine on her way home from work. An hour later, she was pacing the floor, the wine chilling. She changed the music on the stereo three times before finally settling on an old folk tune collection.

Phil was nearly as nervous as Maggie. He couldn't understand how he could care about her so much, yet be so apprehensive. He wished he had made love to her last weekend at the lake, like he'd desperately wanted to. He'd been regretting it all week. He could have taken her to some secluded spot, or even brought her back to his place for the night. Having a week to think about it was driving him nuts. Planning the seduction played on his mind. He could definitely see the advantages of spontaneity.

As he parked in front of Maggie's building, he reached into his pocket to be sure he'd come prepared. He grabbed the bag on the seat beside him. How he remembered to pick up the food he wasn't sure. As much as he enjoyed good food, it was not a top priority tonight.

She looked so good; Phil could hardly put the bag of food down quickly enough to reach for her. He didn't want to appear overanxious, but when he swept her into an embrace, there was no tempering his reaction. "Hello Maggie Love," he whispered. His mouth on hers cut off her greeting.

The kiss was like a long cool drink of water after an agonizing walk in the blistering sun. The relief was instant and mutual, the sexual tension cushioned by the humor of the moment.

Maggie began laughing first. "It's been a long week, hasn't it?"

Phil groaned, nuzzling her neck and ear. "I'm not sure why I bothered with food. You taste good enough to eat."

"I don't think I could eat right now either. My stomach has been fluttering all afternoon."

"Mine too."

"In that case, how about a glass of wine?"

Daylight surrendered to twilight. The food boxes were discarded, the candles burnt low and the wine bottle was almost empty while Maggie and Phil sat gazing at each other, comfortable with each

111

other again but expectant. The sexual undercurrent, thick and soothing as after dinner liqueur, had been building all evening.

His thumb gently traced the bumpy ridge across her knuckles, her hand in his. She'd kicked off her sandals and her bare foot cruised seductively up and down the calf of Phil's pant leg. She needed to touch him to reassure herself of his reality, that he was here because he loved her.

Phil rose to change the music on the stereo. Meanwhile, Maggie snuffed out the candles. She came up behind him, slipped her arms around his waist, just as Hagood Hardy began to play softly. She could feel the muscles along his spine and shoulders tighten through the cool cotton of his shirt. Gently, she rested her cheek against his back and swayed to the music. "Relax, Phil," she murmured.

He covered her hands with his and after several deep breaths, he drew her around to face him. "I've waited a long time for this." He wanted this night to be perfect.

"Mmm... hmm," was her only reply. She kept her arms around his middle.

He linked his hands behind her back and rested his cheek on the top of her head. The music was setting a slow deliberate pace. The tautness across his back vanished beneath her caressing fingers.

With her cheek against his chest, Maggie could smell his cologne, Colors, the one she loved. She inhaled deeply, a scent that was a mixture of the cologne, soap, and Phil's masculinity. She had the urge to open his shirt and rub her face across the silkiness of his chest.

Very slowly, Maggie tugged at the back of his shirt to free it from the confines of his jeans. Inch by unhurried inch it came loose. His muscles tensed anew as she slid her hands gingerly up the warm flesh of his back, over the solid ridges she found there. She could feel the hardness of him through their clothing as he pressed her hips against his. His lips found hers, hungry and fierce. She answered with matching intensity.

The need rose to Maggie's throat like the cork in a wine bottle. All that escaped was a low moan. She could feel the heat spreading, his mouth lighting a fire with kisses along her neck, down her shoulders.

He pulled aside the straps of her dress and felt the warmth trapped there with his lips. Her skin tasted slightly woodsy like she smelled.

Time was suspended as wave after wave of sensation threatened to buckle her knees. Maggie reached for his hand and led him toward her bedroom, switching off the lights as she went. She left the music playing. On the bedside table a lamp shed a soft golden glow. She wished she'd remembered to turn it off earlier. The thought of his seeing the enormity of her scared the daylights out of her for a second. Should she turn it off? Then she remembered her vow, to put her self-consciousness away for tonight. If he really loved her, he'd love all of her.

Maggie watched the shadows darken Phil's eyes. She remembered her earlier warning – never trust a man with brown eyes. It made her smile now. Those same brown eyes that she initially found intimidating were now warm, loving, and searching. She would trust him to love her tonight. She refused to consider anything beyond this one night.

He dropped her hand, crossed the room and turned off the lamp. The only light now was the streak of moonlight cast diagonally across the room through the tied-back drapes.

Her love for him swelled. Tears brimmed in her eyes. She was glad he couldn't see her tears, how touched she was by this simple gesture. He was making this as comfortable for her as possible. How could she do anything but love him, brown eyes and all?

Watching him in the muted light, Maggie began to unbutton her dress, but Phil's hand stopped her.

"Allow me, Maggie." He took over the task. Button by button she was revealed to him till only her bra and panties remained. Tossing the dress onto the chair, his fingers skimmed down her shoulders till he grasped her hands. He placed them around his waist, lowering his mouth to the curve of her breast. He teased and tickled through the barrier of clothing till he felt the bead at the swell of her breast harden beneath his attention. Impatience and the need to touch her full breasts became acute. He unfastened the bra, flinging it toward the chair. Both hands were filled with her, warm and soft, the nipples erect and proud. He was awed.

113

A new wave of pleasure swept through her when he touched and tasted. His fingers seared the places he grazed, awakening an eagerness in Maggie. She helped him out of his clothes till they faced each other naked.

He was breathtaking, a massive and muscled chest with a generous sprinkling of golden brown hair trailing in a V toward his manhood. Maggie discovered he was a finely sculpted chunk of man, his form and features pleasing to her eye in the subdued light. There were no sharp angles or protruding bones. He was as padded as she.

She was unaware that while she was tracking the ridges and contours of his body with her fingertips, he was assessing hers in the dim moonlight. He too was pleased. She was all woman, soft and curves. Someday soon he hoped she would feel secure enough in his love to leave the lights on. But for now he would respect her limitations. He eased them both onto the bed.

He loved the generosity of her breasts. This was new to him. He'd never made love to a woman as amply endowed as Maggie. His lips traveled the curve around to her underarm and back, teasing. At the tip, he brushed his tongue across the surface, feeling the hardness. He took it into his mouth, pulling gently. He nibbled, nipped and nuzzled.

Maggie gripped his shoulders, a gasp escaping her lips. She was losing the awareness of her surroundings, succumbing to the ripples of pleasure. Nothing else existed – just now – with Phil.

The urgency built in Phil's loins as she responded to his loving. But he'd waited a long time for this moment. It was not one to hurry. They had all night. He planned to savor this experience. There would be time enough for his satisfaction later. He knew this was not a trivial step for Maggie. He needed her to know that he cherished her body just as she was, like he'd already come to love the rest of her – her mind, sense of humor and honesty. He loved the fullness of her. His satisfaction would not be complete till she knew that.

The soft silky underside of her arms commanded his attention. He placed her hands above her head and with his mouth alternated from one arm to the other, stopping in between to delve into her warm inviting mouth. He felt her reserve slip away as arousal mounted.

Twilight became night. Maggie could scarcely believe what was happening to her. Her insides were melting as jolt after jolt seared through her. She explored the planes and ridges of his body as he tantalized hers. His hands and mouth took her to the edge of unfathomable pleasure. She wondered how much more stimulation she could stand before she burst into flame.

When neither could stand the torture of titillation any longer, he slid into her. She was hot with passion, liquid and welcoming. A sense of rightness and naturalness enveloped them. Shyness and hesitancy were abandoned. His lips bruised hers as he drove ever deeper, crushing her beneath him. Her fingers dug into the flesh of his shoulders, back and buttocks. Gentleness lost to urgency. Previously known limits of exhilaration and endurance were propelled to new heights. Finally, his throbbing hardness exploded in answer to the spasms that rocketed Maggie over the edge of sensibility to a mindless place where only light and pure joy resided.

They lay facing each other, moonlight illuminating their sated glistening shapes. He brushed her hair off her shoulder to behind her ear so he could plant a kiss there. "You're incredible, Maggie. The more I know you, the more intrigued I become." He nuzzled the spot he'd found on her neck that made her twitch when he touched it with his lips.

Maggie touched his lips with hers, resting her hand along his cheek and whispered, "I never believed I could love anyone like I love you right now. Thank you, Phil." Her churning emotions choked off any further words.

"The pleasure was all mine," he replied, testing her twitch reaction till she began to giggle.

"Hardly. But, now it's my turn," she promised as she rolled him onto his stomach. Phil complied, offering no resistance.

She began an exploration of her own, which started with trailing kisses along his shoulders, feather light caresses along his ribs, gently gnawing his earlobe. He buried his face in the pillow to stifle his moans. She felt his muscles tense and excitement build.

After they'd made love, he had felt relaxed, dreamy and totally satisfied, about to drift into a deep slumber. He thought Maggie felt the same. But perhaps not.

Beneath her hands and mouth his body was tensing and hardening once again. Phil clutched the pillow tightly over his face. All thoughts of sleep vanished as he traveled with her to the brink of arousal. His need for her was immediate and imperative again.

Maggie was amazed to feel the response she could evoke in Phil. He totally gave himself over to the present moment and simply enjoyed, without embarrassment or restraint. It gave her confidence to proceed, to let down her own barriers a bit further. Her touch along the backs of his knees elicited an instinctive reaction. His foot came up off the bed. A feathery stroke along the back of his thighs made his toes curl. The soles of his feet were broad and smooth, the size of small snowshoes.

Phil raised his face from the pillow, looked over his shoulder with a word of warning. "Don't tickle."

"Are you ticklish, Phil?" she asked innocently. "Let's see."

In a flash, Phil rolled over and seized her about the waist, wrestling her onto her back. She offered little resistance. The kibitzing was short lived. He swept her hair off her face and planted soft kisses there instead.

His tenderness made him more precious to Maggie than his strength. To know this man could be so tender melted her heart. She reached up and circled his neck with her arms and gave herself fully to his loving.

They moved together in deliberate and unhurried fashion. Their rhythm was steady. Maggie couldn't believe that the need for him was there again so soon. How could he know just what to do to make her groan and gasp and murmur unintelligible words? She did not care as the pace accelerated. They drove each other slightly senseless. Release came swift and shattering. Finally, exhaustion claimed their weary limbs as the first glimmer of a new day appeared on the horizon.

CHAPTER TWENTY

The sound of glass smashing launched Maggie from slumber to full alert instantly. Her heart hammered as adrenaline pumped through her veins. She was out of bed in a flash. Phil was gone. She snatched her robe. Rounding the corner into the dining room, she saw Phil, clad only in a pink bath towel, gingerly picking his way through the glass shards scattered across the kitchen floor.

"Stop!" she ordered holding up one hand while the other clutched her robe together. "Let me slip on my shoes. Then I'll get the broom before you cut your feet to shreds." She slid her feet into her sandals by the door.

Phil halted. "Sorry I woke you, Maggie Love." He grinned sheepishly. "I was going to surprise you with breakfast, but in an attempt to be quiet, I've managed to startle you. I dropped a glass."

"It's okay."

"Sorry about the glass."

Scooping the remains into the garbage can, she stopped in front of Phil, standing still as a mannequin on tiptoe. "Don't worry about the glass. Being served breakfast in bed is worth one little old glass." Turning and sauntering out of the kitchen Maggie added playfully over her shoulder, "This never happened and I'm still sleeping." She hesitated at the doorway and turned around, trying to be serious. "I've never seen that pink towel look better."

She could hear him laughing and muttering to himself as he finished preparing the tray. Dropping her robe at the foot of the bed, Maggie snuggled back into bed. With her eyes shut, she breathed deeply the new scent on her pillows. She realized that it smelled faintly like it used to, plus a new scent. Unmistakably Phil. She allowed the smell of him to take her back to last night. Remembering their passion in the light of day was every bit as satisfying as it had been last night.

Almost instinctively, Maggie felt for the thickened area of her left breast. It seemed the same as yesterday. If Phil had noticed, he didn't indicate. She wished she'd thought to slip into a nightgown before she crawled back into bed.

Clearing his throat loudly, Phil announced, "Breakfast is served."

Maggie smiled at the sight of him. He looked so contradictory; all muscle and hulk in a fluffy pink towel. She sat up yoga style, pulling the sheet up over her breasts and tucked it under her arms. She smoothed the tangled bedding to make a place for the tray. The coffee smelled heavenly.

Phil sat cross-legged, facing her, with the tray between them. He leaned over and kissed her. "Good morning. Did you sleep well?" he asked, his eyes twinkling, a smile deepening his dimples.

"Like a baby," she answered, returning the smile, relaxed and feeling every inch a contented woman. She took his whiskered face in her hands and planted a kiss firmly on his lips. "Thank you."

"The pleasure was mine, Maggie Love." The reality of the fact that he'd spent the night making love to this earthy, sexy woman caused a lump to rise in his throat. He caressed her shoulders and let a finger trail down to where the sheet covered her, tugging at it gently, loosening it enough to slip his hand under her warm breast. The need for her hit him squarely in the chest and rushed to his loins. His body responded immediately. "Maybe we should let the coffee cool a bit," he suggested, his eyes never leaving hers. He was already moving the tray to the floor. Her eyes were glazed, and he knew coffee wasn't Maggie's immediate concern either.

His mouth crushed down on hers, claiming the territory as his own. His tongue speared hers sending streams of hot liquid down through Maggie's core. With one jerk, the sheet ceased to be a barrier. Maggie caught the end of the towel and flipped it on the floor. Skin to skin and mouth to mouth, desire was rapidly renewed like an ember burst into flame at the slightest encouragement. Touching, tasting they tousled.

There was no finesse this time. Just a demanding urgency to be fulfilled. She arched to meet his plunge. His hands were rough as they kneaded and squeezed. His whiskers grated on her face, neck and breasts. She gasped when he took the tip of one in his mouth and tugged. Her nails dug into the straining muscles of his torso, the wave they were riding beginning to peak. They rocked and reeled to dizzying heights, fast and furious. The delirious wave broke and they crashed together, spent and sweating.

Phil rolled off her, worried that his weight was too much for her to bear. His breathing had not yet returned to normal. Slowly, he picked up her limp hand and brought it to his lips. He kissed the palm, then turned it over and kissed the knuckles and tips. "That was much better than coffee to start the day, don't you think?"

Maggie was enjoying the lazy tremors of their lovemaking that echoed through her. Languidly she turned to face him, stroking his whiskered face. "Infinitely better."

Silently they watched the shadows dancing across the ceiling. The world outside went about its business as though nothing had changed, but Phil and Maggie knew differently. Everything had changed.

"I don't think I've ever been happier than I am at this very minute," Maggie quietly declared. "Even in my daydreams I never imagined a moment quite like this one." All worries were pushed out of her immediate consciousness. The only reality was this sweet sleepy state and this burly brown-eyed man stretched out at her side.

"M-mm."

Just when Maggie thought he'd dozed off, he sat up, reached over the side of the bed and retrieved the tray. With a look of complete contentment, he said, "Now coffee."

The roller coaster ride lasted all weekend, the arousing, the growing familiar and comfortable. They shared secrets, learned idiosyncrasies and marveled at uniqueness of the other.

Phil found out that Maggie loved toasted bagels with butter and honey for breakfast Sunday mornings; that she loved to sleep with the window open; that she could and would whip up a batch of blueberry muffins because he expressed a craving for one at two o'clock in the morning. He was amazed to discover that she directed her own financial investments and that when she got dressed she always put on sock, shoe, sock, shoe, instead of sock, sock; shoe, shoe.

He left his clothes in a heap on the bathroom floor. Maggie realized that it didn't offend or annoy her but rather reminded her of home, growing up with her two brothers. He read in the bathroom, liked his music loud, his coffee strong and plump feather pillows. He had a faint scar under his right arm along his ribcage. When he was eight years old, he'd fallen out of a poplar tree landing on a rock at Little Bear Lake.

Phil suggested they revisit the lake the following weekend. His camping gear wasn't sophisticated but adequate. He didn't have a camper, but he did have a deluxe tent. Was she interested?

Maggie considered for a moment, then answered, "Great! What should I bring?"

On Sunday afternoon, they snuggled on the couch, each with a pad and pen making their respective lists. Phil would bring all the camping equipment, while Maggie supplied the groceries. This was high adventure for Maggie. This would be real camping, a tent instead of a cabin or her parents' camper.

For Phil it was a chance to revisit the place where most of his summers as a boy were spent. For both of them, it would be an opportunity for testing and trying on this new relationship.

Their excitement grew as the camping trip began to take shape. By the time Phil left for home Sunday evening, the plan was to meet at the Hanson Lake corner at six-thirty the following Friday evening. They would travel together from there.

"I wish we could go tomorrow," Maggie said against Phil's shirt, as he held her in his arms to say good-bye. "I can hardly wait."

"Me too," he sighed and kissed the top of her head. "This has been the best weekend of my life. It's hard to believe that just two days ago I was so nervous about being here with you, I was shaking in my boots. Now this feels so good, so right, I don't want to leave."

"It has been a grand time, hasn't it?" She looked up into his chocolate brown eyes. She would remember the love she saw there in the days to come when she would miss him terribly. These memories would sustain her till Friday. She stroked his back and shoulders. She loved the feel of him, the smell that was his own, the twitching of his right eye when he was nervous.

Maggie's apartment felt empty all week. It was hard to believe that Phil had made such an impact in the couple days they'd spent together. She found the nights especially lonely.

They talked on the phone every day, often several times a day. Once in a while, it was a reminder to bring something or a question, but these were mostly excuses to hear the other's voice.

Friday finally arrived. Maggie had told Joan only that she was going out of town for the weekend. Joan didn't ask and Maggie didn't volunteer any further information. She caught herself several times during the day, fantasizing about the weekend. She only hoped that she hadn't made any serious errors at work. She rationalized that everyone was preoccupied once in a while. It was her turn.

Phil was waiting for her at the corner when she arrived. Before she could carry any of the supplies to his Jimmy, he scooped her into his arms and kissed her hungrily. It renewed their passion, which had been simmering all week. Because it was daylight and they were in plain view of traffic, they refrained from tearing each other's clothes off.

Maggie was backed up against his vehicle and could distinctly feel the pressure of his growing hardness. It left her breathless.

Gasping for air, she said, "Let's get going and get that tent set up."

Phil saw that she was as anxious as he. "Yes, let's."

The farmland soon disappeared and the forest welcomed them. The stately spruce and majestic pines provided a warm cocoon. The rest of the way, they gazed longingly at each other and touched constantly in anticipation. Maggie just wanted to burrow into his arms and shut out the rest of the world. She longed to feel secure, satisfied, and totally feminine in his embrace. When her nerve endings were all humming, it was easy to nearly forget about the terrorizing lump.

They picked a secluded campsite totally surrounded by pines and young poplars. Phil noticed when he squatted down to pound in the tent pegs that if he got down far enough, he was afforded an incredible view of the sun setting over the lake. So before the tent was erected, they lay on it, side by side on their bellies, and enjoyed the shimmering blaze of colors – oranges, strong reds, and a brilliant yellow globe swirled against a bright blue canvas. They were awed by the majesty of nature's display.

They could hear other campers in the distance, but their spot remained private. Fishing boats returning with their catch were faintly audible. The bird chorus launched into their night songs.

Maggie was aware of none of nature's beauty outside the tent. Inside, she was clinging to the smallest shred of reality. Her entire body was singing its own song to a tune masterfully crafted by Phil. Each touch added another melody to the chorus. She felt that if she allowed herself, she could slip into a state of pure joy that was elemental and earthy. She knew that to feel like this was a gift. The intimacy was unlike anything she'd ever experienced before. It wasn't just the physical meeting of two bodies, but the union of her soul with its mate.

Maggie was experimenting with Phil's dimples. The sensation of running her tongue lightly along his cheek, only to have it drop off into the crevice of his dimple, was erotic. He was lying on his side with one arm under his head, trying hard not to shudder.

"Quit that, Maggie. It tickles."

To distract her, he cupped her breast with his free hand and began to gently caressed it. "I love the abundance of you," he said. "Feels like warm creamy white silk. I don't think I will ever get enough of you."

What would he say if he knew that she might very well lose that breast if the lump proved to be cancerous? Would he still want to look at her as he was now? Touch her? Make love to her with the passion they had just experienced? She took a deep breath, pushed those thoughts from her mind to concentrate on what was happening in the depths of her body. She allowed him to sweep her along the paths of sublime sensation, relaxing and savoring the exploration process.

Maggie woke with a start when a cold raindrop landed on her bare thigh. A rumble sounded from somewhere across the lake. She sat up and looked around to get her bearings. Phil was naked, sprawled across the sleeping bag beside her, sound asleep. She reached to close the flaps on her side of the tent, to keep out the rain. She sat with her knees drawn up, a blanket around her shoulders, and watched the lightning through the window on the opposite side of the tent.

The performance was awesome. It flared and danced, lighting up the entire sky. The leaves on the poplar trees glistened wet and silver like shiny new fifty-cent pieces. Inside the tent, the light played along the lines of Phil's shoulders and legs, the planes of his back and the curves of his buttocks. She was absorbed in studying his shape when a clap of thunder shook the earth beneath them.

Phil flew to his feet in alarm. His head nearly went through the tent roof, halted abruptly when he rapped it hard against a roof support. He yelped in surprise as much as in pain.

Maggie burst out laughing when she realized he wasn't injured, only startled. He sat down cross-legged on his sleeping bag, clutching his head.

"What the hell was that?" he asked, rubbing his head.

"Come here," she said, motioning him closer. "It was only thunder. Let me see if you're bleeding." She dug out a flashlight to have a better look. She was relieved to find no blood but a small budding knob. She kissed it carefully. "Does that feel better?"

"I'm sure I'll forget all about it if you keep that up," he assured her, snuggling closer.

They huddled together under Maggie's blanket, watching Mother Nature's late show. The gentle holding and caresses became arousing. Slowly, steadily like the rain outside, their senses quickened. There was no hurry, no urgency; just the continual stirring that pleaded for completion. The coming together was as stimulating as it was soothing. They made love for what seemed like hours, in tune with each other and the subtle pulse of the earth.

CHAPTER TWENTY-ONE

An attempt had been made to make this dreaded place bearable, Maggie observed as she sat in the tiny waiting room. The windows directly opposite overlooked a courtyard. Cherry red petunias, snowy white peonies and sturdy marigolds were tucked in under the flowering ornamental plums and apple trees. Brilliant sunflower yellow cushions were tossed on the cornflower blue couch and chairs. The glass table held the latest issues of *Chatelaine*, *Canadian Living* and *Readers Digest*. Despite all this, it was still the mammography department of St. Elizabeth's Hospital in Prince Albert. The odor of industrial strength antiseptic permeated the place.

Maggie wondered how many women had passed through this room without even noticing the surroundings. She was making a conscious effort to keep her imagination in check. Without such diligence she would find herself projected into the future, dealing with the horrors of breast cancer or she would find herself in the past reliving the time she waited with her father for the results of her mother's surgery. Neither was beneficial. Maggie, hugging close the green garment she'd been given to wear, crossed to the window and stared out at the courtyard.

She let her thoughts wander back to her days with Phil. The days they'd spent together seemed like precious gems, especially here where the worry and tension in the air was real and frigid. She could almost reach out and touch it. Fear – as dark, thick and nauseating as unrefined crude oil.

Maggie was beginning to understand why she loved him. He encouraged her to be who she was – strong, skilled, and self-sufficient. But he loved her soft, caring and tender side as well. He appreciated her humor and spontaneity.

It troubled her periodically that she never mentioned the lump in her breast or the upcoming mammography to him. After all, wasn't she the one who demanded honesty? Then, on the other hand, she thought he would understand her need to get through this on her own, to prove she was strong enough to withstand what life threw her direction. Besides, what was the point in telling him that they would mutilate her body if surgery proved unnecessary? Just when it seemed that he accepted and loved her just as she was, this happened.

She was grateful for their time together. They would be the memories she would hold onto if he rejected her later. She believed he might if the tests were positive and she needed surgery and treatment. Her chances for starting a family would disappear with her breast, she believed.

"Miss Mills," a cheery voice called. "Would you follow me please?"

The voice belonged to a woman about Maggie's age. She appeared to be cheerfully competent as she showed Maggie into the breast imaging room. Her makeup didn't quite hide the shadows under her eyes. Maggie speculated that she had a family, maybe a cranky baby that kept her up last night. Her shoulder length hair was pulled back and held in a clip. Over the soft pink pants and top she wore a brightly flowered jacket which flared as she rounded the desk. She indicated a seat to Maggie.

"My name is Mavis Webber, your mammography technician. Just a few questions first, Miss Mills, before we begin." She smiled, noting the uncertainty on Maggie's face. "Is this your first mammogram?"

Maggie nodded, clutching the flimsy top tightly shut.

Mavis scribbled on the forms in front of her as she established Maggie's general health, the reason for the mammogram, and her medical history. "We will mark the spot on your left breast to ensure we get good shots of that area."

Maggie surveyed the room. In the center of the room stood a machine with an opaque glass surface, levers and knobs. Beside it was a machine with a screen above it and a bulb-shaped apparatus attached to a cable.

Against the window, with the shades drawn, were two chairs. The sunflower and blue design added a sunny atmosphere. A wallpaper border of sunflowers leaning in the breeze ran around the room at waist level. Off near the door was an enclosed area that resembled a glass phone booth with a panel of instruments. It seemed a rather pleasant room, not one where Maggie could receive the most devastating news of her life.

Mavis directed Maggie to stand on the side of the machine with the flat glass surface. "Here, Maggie, we'll strap this lead apron on you to protect your ovaries and such from radiation." Mavis snugged it around Maggie's waist. "Now, slip off your top. Rest your right breast on the plate." Maggie followed her directions. The plate felt icy cold to her warm flesh, sending a shiver up her arms. Mavis adjusted it to Maggie's height. "Lean your shoulder in. Just like that. Now, we'll apply the pressure," as she brought down the huge plastic clamp. She increased the pressure until Maggie was positive everything in her breast would be squashed flat as a pancake. It wasn't extremely painful, but rather, very uncomfortable.

"Hold it." Mavis slipped into the booth when she was sure of a perfect picture. "Hold your breath."

Seconds later Mavis returned to readjust the plates so that the pressure was applied vertically to Maggie's breast.

Mavis marked an X on the spot where the lump could be felt on her left breast and the entire procedure was repeated. When they were finished, Mavis excused herself, asking Maggie to have a seat and wait a minute or two until the radiologist had a look at the x-rays.

Maggie sat looking at the sunflowers, trying to keep a tight rein on the panic rising in her throat. She held fast to the green hospital garb covering her and rocked. The two minutes felt like two hours.

Mavis returned. Maggie tried to read her face for an indication of the results. She could not. "The radiologist would like an ultrasound of your left breast, so we might as well do that before you get dressed."

She motioned Maggie to assume her former position behind the machine. She pushed the overhead part further out of the way and proceeded to turn knobs and dials on the machine with the screen. "This won't hurt at all. Place your breast on this plate again and I'll put some gel on it to make this slide easier," she said waving the bulb-like instrument with the cable. Mavis explained that it was a transducer. It sent the sound waves into the tissue that would appear as images on the screen. She smeared both Maggie's breast and the end of the bulb with cool gel. Slowly Mavis moved the transducer across her breast, watching the images dance across the screen. Intermittently, she would stop, holding still and press a button. When she was finished, Mavis reached for a towel for Maggie to wipe off the gel.

"If you'd like to get dressed and wait, Miss Mills, we'll call you with the results in a few minutes."

Maggie took several deep breaths to ease the tightness in her chest as she waited. Suddenly, she wished she'd asked Phil to come with her. His warm, firm grip would have been reassuring and supportive. How silly! He had classes and this was a routine procedure. Hundreds of women underwent this test everyday without being traumatized. So could she! She was a realist, preferring to know what she was up against. The ostrich syndrome never worked for her. It ate away at her till her stomach ached.

Mavis returned with a file tucked under her arm. "Miss Mills, would you like to step in here?" She stood holding open the door to the imaging room. Maggie entered. Mavis crossed over to a panel on the wall by her desk and flipped a switch. The panel lit up and she thrust x-rays into a clip along the top.

"See this," Mavis instructed as she pointed to a whitish area. There is definitely a lump of some sort here. Here it is from another angle. It's about the size of a marble," she said, pointing to another x-ray.

Maggie found it hard to believe these x-rays represented her breasts. There were lines and spots of varying degrees of black and white. In a high thin voice, she asked, "Can you tell what it is?"

Mavis sat on the corner of her desk and faced Maggie. "No, we can't. We'll send these results to Dr...." She flipped open the file and read, "Dr. Staeger. She will schedule you for a biopsy. The results of that will show whether or not it is malignant." She paused for a moment, then continued. "You realize, Miss Mills, that eight or nine out of every ten lumps are benign. So wait until you have the results of the biopsy to worry. Okay?"

"Yes, of course. Thank you."

Maggie left instructing herself to act normal. Nobody was staring. Nobody could see the lump. She walked to the parking lot, unlocked the door and waited a few minutes, allowing the heat trapped inside to escape. The beauty and cheery sunshine of the early summer day was lost on Maggie.

Driving out, she decided she could really use a coffee. She'd given up coffee for the past three days. The brochure Dr. Staeger had given her stated the procedure would be less painful without caffeine in her system. But now she would indulge. It might calm her jangled nerves.

She drove to the mall and parked as if she'd been switched to automatic pilot. Her brain felt stuck, unable to function. Her feet carried her to the food court, where she ordered a large coffee, hoping the caffeine would return her system to normal.

The dark rich brew smelled wonderful as she inhaled deeply. It was second only to the first sip. Her taste buds burst to life. This was maybe the best coffee she'd ever tasted, other than the early morning coffee or the campfire coffee shared with Phil. But then, it wasn't so much the coffee as it was the company on those occasions.

She was enjoying her second cup of delicious coffee, watching the mall shoppers saunter by. Suddenly, there he was. Maggie blinked to be sure she wasn't hallucinating. It was Phil. She'd recognize his profile anywhere.

Phil was leaning on the counter in the jewelry store across from where she sat. He was laughing and talking to a woman leaning on the counter with him, their shoulders touching, heads together. He pointed to something in the display case and a clerk retrieved it for the two of them to examine. And then another item and another. They were looking at rings! The woman slipped one onto her finger and showed Phil. The tittering continued as she tried on several more and Maggie passed into a state of shock. Several minutes later, a woman emerged from the back of the store, handed Phil a package and they turned to leave.

Maggie was praying the floor would open up and swallow her. She watched unbelieving as he held open the door for her, placed his hand on her back and steered her toward the mall exit. They were obviously enjoying themselves, sharing what appeared to be a private moment.

Maggie sat frozen, only her eyes following their progress as they left the mall. Phil had not seen her.

Maggie wasn't sure what it was she felt. Her emotions flipped from neutral to chaos when the shock faded and her brain replayed and digested the scene. Bewilderment – she had slept with him only a few nights ago. Now, here he was, with another woman in a jewelry store. And, they were shopping for rings. Jealousy – this woman was short, blonde and probably a size ten. Anger – how dare he use her? Now that he'd been to bed with her, had he decided her large size was not for him after all? How could he do this to her? Especially today, when she needed his strength and support.

She'd been struggling for control all day. Tears welled up, her coffee forgotten. Sleep had evaded her last night. This was the final straw. She made it to her car before the dam burst. With her forehead resting on the steering wheel, a torrent of tears gushed forth. She didn't even bother wiping her eyes but just allowed the stream to fall onto the steering wheel and then into her lap, staining her blue pants a dark navy.

She had planned to call Phil after school, maybe have supper with him before she drove home. If he asked why she was in Prince Albert, she would tell him she had an appointment and hope he didn't pursue the matter. Or maybe she secretly hoped he would. If he did, she planned to tell him the truth. But she hoped she wouldn't have to tell him until she knew the results of the biopsy.

Instead she drove home crying, hungry, angry, humiliated and miserable. She'd never felt more unlovable and alone in her life.

By the time she reached her apartment, she thought she'd cried herself out, but when she walked into her bedroom, she pictured Phil reclining against the propped up pillows with his coffee cup resting on his stomach. Maggie flung herself on the bed and wept again. She cried for her broken heart; she cried for the breast she might lose; she cried for her shattered trust; she cried for a relationship that could have been. Sleep finally overtook her.

It was dark when the ringing of the phone woke her. She groaned as she rolled over. The movement brought the pain slamming into her head, her eyes throbbing. She reached for the phone. The clock glared ten twenty-five.

"Hello," she croaked, her throat sore.

"Hi, Maggie Love. You sound hoarse. Were you sleeping?" Phil greeted her good-naturedly as usual.

How could he pretend everything was normal, she wondered.

"Yeah, I was sleeping," she answered without feeling.

"Are you okay?" he asked.

Now he sounded concerned. What a phony two-timing jerk!

"No, I'm just fine," she replied frostily. Her defensive barriers rose immediately. She wasn't going to give him the satisfaction of dumping her for some skinny wench. She'd do the dumping first. Maybe he'd been carrying on with both of them at the same time. Well, let him have her! She never should have trusted a brown-eyed man! "Were you looking at rings in Booth's Jewelers this afternoon?" she asked.

"Yes, I was there with…"

The 'yes' echoed through her brain like a rifle shot. Before he could finish, she coldly interrupted, "I've been doing a lot of thinking since the weekend and I don't think things are going to work out between us."

"Whoa, Maggie, what are you talking about? I thought…" He sounded confused. He probably didn't think she would ever find out about his other woman. He was no doubt sleeping with her too.

She interrupted again, this time frigidly, "I've decided we shouldn't see each other anymore… before this goes any further. Good-bye, Phil."

"Maggie, just a…"

She couldn't stand to hear any of his lies. Maggie slammed the phone down before she started to cry again.

Within seconds it rang again. She ignored it. It rang every five minutes till finally Maggie turned it off and crawled into a steaming tub of water to soak away some the aches. The water wasn't nearly hot enough to dissolve the deep aching pain within her. She went to bed, knowing that she would survive without Phil. She had more important things to deal with, maybe life and death issues. She resolved to direct her energy toward that instead. But how she ached for his soothing, comforting arms around her. It was hours before slumber brought relief from her torment.

CHAPTER TWENTY-TWO

The next morning, Maggie called Dr. Staeger's office after Joan left her desk to get coffee. She made an appointment for the following Tuesday. Just as she was hanging up, Joan popped her head back into the office. She picked up her purse and headed for the bathroom. Maggie wondered how much of the conversation she'd heard. She was too exhausted to care, nor did she have the energy to explain.

Mentally, she thanked Joan for not pressuring her to talk. She wondered if Joan knew about her and Phil. Maybe he'd called them when Maggie refused to answer her phone last night. Maybe she even knew about this other woman. But she would not ask!

From the look on Maggie's face when Joan arrived at work, Joan knew something was dreadfully wrong, but she knew Maggie well enough to know that pressing for details would backfire. When Maggie was ready, she would share, but not till then. In the meantime, Joan made a mental list of possibilities. The return of Lenore Mill's cancer headed the list. Her brother-in-law Phil was number two on her list.

The weekend ahead was predicted to be sunny and unusually warm for June. By Friday, Maggie was numb, and the day passed in a blur. She needed to keep her mind from wandering into the minefield of her emotions, where desolation and despair certainly awaited.

After work, Maggie loaded up with videos. She popped a huge bowl of popcorn and tried to relax. Instead she became more anxious and troubled as the phone rang every half hour, and the temperature in her apartment rose to sweltering.

She tried telling herself that it was all for the best despite the pain that racked her body every time she thought of him and what they'd had together. The loss left such a hollow in her gut. It felt as though someone had carved out her insides with a scoop shovel. She curled up into the fetal position in an attempt to protect herself from the pain. She couldn't remember ever being hurt so deeply. Even when Richard left, it hadn't hurt this much, partly because she now realized that she hadn't been entirely committed to him in the first place. This time she'd given herself totally to this relationship, and the betrayal was excruciating. With Phil, she had experienced sheer joy that rendered her mindless, and now he was the cause of her deepest agony.

She had to find a way to mend her heart, her shattered self-image and her trust in her own instincts. She needed to do it quickly if she wanted to avoid questions from her family and friends. Furthermore, she would need all her resources to face the biopsy and whatever followed.

Saturday she decided to go to the movies. The theatre was air-conditioned, and she didn't have to listen to the phone ring. A horror film was playing, so she sat with her eyes closed, wondering if Phil was calling. Why he was still calling baffled her, especially when he had this new love.

Sunday she dragged her bulk out of bed, got dressed and went to eleven o'clock church service. It felt comforting to be there. Regardless of what changed in her life, she knew this place would always be here for her. This church and family would provide the stability she so badly needed right now. She steeled herself to disguise her pain so her parents wouldn't cross-examine her. She took the risk and stopped by their house to see if they would like to go out for brunch. She needed their familiar faces and voices. Maggie believed that even the small comforts would soothe her wounded psyche.

They hurriedly changed and went with Maggie. Both Lenore and Jackson sensed something was amiss. Neither mentioned a word, for fear of having their heads chewed off. Brunch was uneventful, with only insignificant chatter.

They knew Maggie would talk when it was right for her. That didn't keep them from worrying or discussing the possible problem once they were safely back home and there was no danger of Maggie overhearing their concerns.

Monday and work finally arrived. Never before had she looked so forward to going to work. Maggie was certain it had been the longest weekend she'd lived through. The phone rang several times Sunday evening. She planned to ignore it until Tuesday. She estimated that by then he would surely give up. It was even more puzzling why he would continue to call anyway. Maybe this was his way of torturing her.

The heat continued into the new week. It seemed everyone was out in the evenings watering gardens, lawns, flowerbeds, baskets and pots in an effort to keep them from wilting under the scorching sun. The weather was the main topic of conversation in coffee shops, stores and business places. It seemed everyone was praying for rain.

Maggie hardly noticed. She felt so miserable she made herself sick and spent a good part of the afternoon in the bathroom. She went home feeling ill, totally drained and somewhat foolish about the cause of her sickness.

She berated herself all evening. She had been content before Phil had come along and messed up her life. There was no reason why she couldn't be again, now that he was gone. Besides, she'd decided after Richard's abandonment that she could live quite nicely without a man in her life. That had worked well for her until she got mixed up with Phil. She should have known better than to trust a man with brown eyes, she reminded herself.

The phone continued to ring, but she had neither the energy nor the desire to speak to anyone, especially Phil. He would soon get the message that she wanted nothing more to do with him and go on with his life and new love.

Rest was what her body cried for and her mind craved. Sleep remained elusive throughout the night. When she did doze off, she was awakened by frantic dreams of running wildly through a forest, lost and alone.

Maggie had told Joan she wouldn't be in the next day, the day that might change her life forever. When the sun came up, she pulled the blinds and curtains in her bedroom and slept soundly for two hours.

Her eyes were hardly open when she realized this was the day her entire future might take a different turn. She dreaded the appointment but at the same time wished it was already history and she knew what she had to face. She wondered how so many changes could occur in just a few weeks. A week ago, she was ecstatically happy and believed she could have a future with the man she loved. There was even a good possibility that they would make a home together and children, she believed. Oh, to have been so gullible and naïve. She had asked one thing of him, honesty, and even that was too much.

Dr. Staeger breezed through the door, chart in hand. She was somewhat subdued today, not her bouncy, jovial self. As she took a seat opposite Maggie's, she opened the file.

"As you probably already know, Maggie, the mammogram and ultrasound were inconclusive."

Fighting for composure, Maggie asked quietly, "Now what?"

"Well, considering your family history, we shouldn't waste any time getting this checked out. Based on this," she said, tapping the reports in front of her, "I would recommend a biopsy as soon as possible. Dr. Wooding in Saskatoon has a very good reputation. We were in the same graduating class from medical school, so I know her personally. If you like, I could call and see how quickly she could see you."

Sounding more calm than she felt, Maggie agreed, "Yes, the sooner the better."

"Give me a minute." Dr. Staeger reached over and gave Maggie's arm a squeeze. "I'll be right back."

A few minutes later, Dr. Staeger returned with a handful of forms. "It's all set for the last Wednesday in June. That was the soonest she could see you. It's only a week away. She'll examine you. She may recommend a needle biopsy or she may decide on a lumpectomy. Together you'll decide what's the best for you. You'll need these," she added, handing the forms to Maggie. "You can get the preliminary tests, the blood work, chest x-ray done here and just take the results with you when you go."

Maggie's mind was whirling. There were suddenly so many things to arrange and consider. "Will she use local anesthetic? Will I be able be able to drive home?"

"Yes. It'll be local, so you could probably drive afterwards. It'll be a bit sore when the anesthetic wears off." After a moment, she added gently, "It might be a good idea to consider taking someone with you, for moral support as well as the driving." Holding up a hand so Maggie wouldn't interrupt, she continued," You don't have to go through this alone, Maggie, unless you choose to, but I certainly wouldn't recommend it."

Maggie saw the concern on her doctor's face. She also knew she would do this on her own because she was alone, very much alone. She needed to know that she was strong enough to face this crisis. Without giving Dr. Staeger a clue about her feelings, Maggie answered politely, "Thank you for your concern. Will I hear the results from you or Dr. Wooding?"

Dr. Staeger could tell by the stubborn set of Maggie's jaw that she was ignoring her advice. There was no point in badgering her. Determination to overcome such an obstacle and a positive attitude often made the difference in whether a patient would recover or not. She'd seen that proven plenty of times. "Dr. Wooding will contact you directly, but her office will send me a copy of the results. Good luck, Maggie."

Luck was something she'd never had much of, Maggie thought as she left the doctor's office. If that was the key ingredient to having a dynamic career she was passionate about or a fulfilling love life, she'd surely missed it. And now, it appeared possible that she had the bad luck to develop cancer as well. In fact, it looked like if it wasn't for the bad luck in her life, she wouldn't have any at all!

CHAPTER TWENTY-THREE

School was dragging to a close. Other years, Phil was like most teachers who anxiously awaited that last day of school before summer vacation. This year, he mechanically went through the motions, hardly noticing the countdown on the staff room calendar. All the other teachers were dealing with their own class problems or student crises, so no one noticed Phil's pain. He did his best to hide it. If anyone had noticed, they would have chalked his unusual behavior up to year-end stress.

He had spent hours, days and now weeks replaying the events of those magical days with Maggie to find the cause of her change of heart. For Phil, the time together had been incredible. He had felt closer to her than he ever had with any other human being, never mind a woman. The sex was the best he'd ever had. He loved Maggie more than he believed it was possible to love anyone. Now she was shutting him out and it felt like his life was over. She had twisted and torn his heart until the will to live was nearly strangled.

At first he was stunned by her cruelty. Then came the disbelief. He would just talk to her and find out what was going on, but she refused to answer his calls. He couldn't get through to her. Anger overwhelmed him. He would just drive to Nipawin, pound on her door and demand an explanation. Better wait till he cooled off and could think clearly. That never happened.

She could rot in hell for all he cared. No one was indispensable, and he could find someone else if he wanted to. But he didn't. The pain grew till he began to question his masculinity. Maybe he just didn't have what it took to please a woman and make her happy. It had happened once before, with Shelley. The difference was that Maggie was nothing like Shelley. Or so he thought. Maybe she didn't know what she wanted either. Maybe he'd scared her by voicing his desire to start a family immediately. After weeks, he still hadn't figured it out. All he knew was that the hurt left him hollow and haggard.

Phil knew he had to talk to someone soon before he gave up on life entirely. He had friends, but he wasn't sure whom he could trust with this dilemma. Jason would be sympathetic, but not especially helpful. That was just Jason. His brother Wayne would be embarrassed. Even though they were brothers, they never discussed intimate stuff. He didn't know any professionals, and he didn't feel comfortable discussing this with a stranger. There was no one on staff he was close to. Ironically, the only person he felt at ease talking to in recent months, was Maggie.

With just three days of school left, Phil's eyes were strained from marking exams and his shoulders ached from the tension of being hunched over at his kitchen table for hours. He stood and stretched till some of the kinks loosened. He checked the clock on the stove – seven-twenty. There was still plenty of daylight left. He had time to whip out to the driving range and hit a few golf balls. That would help work off some of his frustration and loosen the tightness in his neck and shoulders. He'd still have plenty of time to finish these last few papers when he returned. He was out the door, his clubs in hand before he could think twice and talk himself out of it.

The golf course was busy. Phil was glad he'd chosen to go to the range instead. Approaching the ball, he settled himself into position, lined up and told himself that the only thing that existed in his world right now was this little ball. So just relax and hit the hell out of it.

"God, what a drive!" a voice came from behind him.

Phil turned. Leaning on his driver was Jon Mills, watching Phil's drive fly past the two hundred and fifty-yard marker. "Jon! What are you doing here?" Phil's surprise was evident.

"Same as you. Relieving some stress by beating the hell out of a little ball. How are you doing?" he asked as he approached Phil, his hand extended. "Good to see you again."

Phil took the offered hand. "Nice to see you too. Do you come here often?"

"Nearly every time I'm in town. But because I don't know when I'll be finished work, it's hard to play a round without booking ahead. Besides, I don't care to play alone, so I come here and hit a few balls instead. How about you? Do you play much?"

Phil was drawn to Jon's easy familiar manner. His coloring was similar to Maggie's, as was his body language, the slight tilt of the head when they asked a question. Both Jon and Maggie carried their large frames with ease and, in Maggie's case, elegance. The physical similarities were such that there was no mistaking them for siblings.

Phil watched him shoot his last few balls. His approach was more relaxed and smooth but had the same result as Phil's tightly wound, intensely concentrated swing. It was relaxing just watching Jon swing a club.

Jon suggested going for a beer after the buckets were empty and the clubs back in their respective bags. Phil learned that Jon, who lived in Saskatoon, traveled the northern half of the province as a sales representative for an electrical supplier. He was generally in Prince Albert overnight once a week, except when he flew to the northern settlements. He did that once a month, so he would be in Prince Albert two nights instead of the regular one.

"Too bad I didn't know that," Phil said, taking a hefty swallow from the sweating mug. "We could have gotten together long before today."

"I did give you a call one night about three weeks ago. There was no answer and then later your line was busy. I thought maybe you were talking to Maggie," he added, pausing to watch Phil's reaction.

Jon was kept posted about the happenings at home on a regular basis. His mother had reported that Phil and Maggie were seeing each other. Lenore had shared with him the fact that it was reported to her that Phil had stayed overnight with Maggie a few weeks ago. Jon was delighted for his sister. She deserved some happiness since that rat Richard left her heart-broken. Good riddance. He liked Phil when he'd met him at the lake. They hadn't known each other in high school, Jon being several years older. But Phil enjoyed sports, so he was okay in Jon's books. Besides, Maggie had seemed happier that weekend at the lake than he'd seen her in years.

Jon was equally aware that something was wrong with Maggie these days. He wondered if it had anything to do with Phil. After Lenore alerted him to the fact that Maggie was acting strangely, he tried calling her several times. She never answered. Now he watched

Phil squirm at the mention of Maggie's name.

"That's possible," he answered tensely, staring into his beer mug. His entire body stiffened. He had almost refused Jon's offer to buy him a beer, afraid Maggie's name would find its way into their conversation. Now it had. How could he bear to talk about Maggie casually?

Jon leaned forward, resting his elbows on the table. "Sorry, man," he said softly. "We can talk about something else." He wasn't sure he wanted to hear about it anyway, but now he knew there was definitely a problem here.

Phil felt like he had the day he'd faced Maggie across her kitchen table. The misery was so overwhelming; the dam was about to burst. He glanced around the bar and found it nearly empty, only a table across the room where three young guys were flirting with the waitress. He wasn't sure if Jon was the right person to talk to or not, but the situation seemed to dictate that perhaps Jon could help him make some sense of Maggie's strange behavior. The tension he thought he'd left on the driving range rolled over him like a tidal wave. It was killing him.

Phil lifted his head and looked at Jon. He saw a kind and compassionate man, and in that instant the decision was made. "No, it's okay. I need to talk to somebody about what's been going on and it might as well be you. Maybe you can help me understand this. You know your sister better than I do."

Jon could see the pain and confusion in Phil's eyes. Whether he wanted to hear this or not, it looked like he was about to. So he settled back in his chair. "I'm not sure I understand Maggie any better than I do women in general, and that's not saying much. But go for it anyway."

By the time Phil had relayed the events of the past few months, leaving out the really intimate details of course, Jon was as baffled by Maggie's actions as was Phil. He believed without a doubt that Phil loved his sister deeply. He could also see that he was a tormented man.

Jon waved at the waitress, indicating they wanted another beer. He leaned forward resting his elbows on the table. "I really don't know what to think, Phil." He reached for a handful of peanuts and pondered while he ate them. "There is one thing I can tell you. Maggie's a very private person. She keeps stuff to herself until she's ready to share it."

The waitress arrived with two mugs of beer. She picked up the empty ones and returned to the bar via the table of young men across the room.

Phil took a swallow from his mug. Setting it down, he flicked his tongue over his upper lip to remove the foam mustache and settled back in his chair. It felt good just to give voice to the thoughts that had been scurrying around inside his head for weeks. He respected Jon for hearing him out. It was also apparent that Maggie had not discussed their relationship with her brother.

"That much I know, too. I'm sure that's why it took us so long to get to where I thought we were."

"She was really hurt by that jerk she was engaged to a few years back. I think maybe that experience has something to do with her inability to trust men easily. Since then she'll snap your head off if you pry into her business. Even if it seems like an innocent question. Mom says she's been worse than ever these past few weeks."

"I just don't understand what's happened," Phil said, searching Jon's face for answers.

"I tried calling her too. She's not answering her phone. There's one thing I do know about Maggie. She's not fickle and she wouldn't purposely hurt anyone. There must be something wrong. A misunderstanding or something."

"But what? And how can I understand this if she won't talk to me?" he pleaded. "How can I make it right if I don't know what's wrong?"

"I'll talk to Mom and see if she knows what's happening with our Maggie."

Phil scribbled his school and home phone numbers on the napkin under his mug and handed it to Jon. "Call me as soon as you find out anything."

When they stood to leave, Phil shook Jon's hand firmly. "Thanks, Jon."

"No problem. Just wish I could have been more help. Maybe next week when I'm in town we could play some golf."

Jon wasted no time in calling home once he reached his hotel room. He'd kicked off his shoes listening to the phone ring. Lenore picked it up on the third ring. After the usual greetings, he told her about running into Phil and their conversation.

"What's going on, Mom?" he asked. "I've tried calling Maggie for weeks too and no answer."

Lenore sighed deeply as she sank into her chair at the kitchen table. "I don't know any more than you do. You know how she gets when I ask questions."

"This is a strange way for her to act if it's a simple misunderstanding, don't you think?" Jon asked. He found women in general a mystery, and his sister more than most right now. That's why Jon loved women in general but none in particular. Once he thought he had one figured out, she ceased to be a challenge, and Jon quickly lost interest.

"I knew she must be serious about that Sanders boy. She never mentioned him, and when I asked her about him, she dismissed it. Said they were just getting to know each other. There's more to it than she's telling." Stretching the phone cord, Lenore poured herself a cup of coffee and sat again.

"I gathered from Phil that he's very serious about Maggie. He really cares for her, Mom."

"That's comforting, Jon. Maybe I'll have to talk with her, try to find out what's up. If I have a head left after our talk, I'll let you know," she laughed.

Lenore knew Jon was concerned about his sister. He was normally the solitary one, minding his own business. As an afterthought, she added, "It was odd, but she called one day to remind me it was time for my check-up. Now how would she know that, I wonder?"

"You know Maggie, Mom. She probably has it written on her calendar to remind you. Who knows? Talk to you again soon."

Lenore decided immediately on a course of action. She checked the time – nine-thirty. She called Maggie. No answer. Grabbing her keys, she stopped in the back yard long enough to tell Jackson where she was going.

Jackson was trimming the grass around the flowerbeds. "If you

142

wait a few minutes till I'm finished, I'll go with you," he said, straightening up.

"No thanks, Jack. I'll go myself. I need to talk to her alone. I won't be long. I'll tell you all about it later.

Before he could protest or ask questions, Lenore was gone. He wondered what the big hurry was.

Maggie, wrapped in a thin green cotton robe, was waiting for the kettle to boil when the doorbell rang. She'd been studying the material Dr. Staeger and Dr. Wooding had given her. She'd read about needle biopsies, lumpectomies and what happened if the mass was found to be cancerous. She was amazed to learn that if it was cancer, her chances with a lumpectomy followed by radiation were as good as a radical mastectomy. Several questions still remained in Maggie's mind, primarily how this would affect her chances of ever having a family.

Her surprise at seeing her mother there was obvious. She held the door open. "Hi Mom. What brings you over?"

Lenore walked in and dropped her keys on the table. "Hi Maggie. I need to talk to you."

"Sure. Have a seat. I was just making a cup of tea." Maggie could tell her mother was upset as she shut the door.

"Make it a pot."

Now she knew this was serious. Maggie gathered up the brochures and pamphlets before her mother could see what they were and placed them in a neat pile on the end of the counter. She brought the teapot and cups to the table, praying it was nothing to do with her mother's health. Maybe she'd been in for her check-up and the cancer had returned. Maggie wasn't sure if she could handle that right now, along with her own problems.

Lenore got to the point at once. She sipped her hot tea and looking straight into Maggie's eyes, she asked, "What's going on, Maggie? You're not your usual self. You're avoiding people who care about you. You're not answering your phone. What's up?"

Maggie knew the only way to keep her problems to herself was to keep to herself as much as possible. Even though she needed her family's support, to be around them would mean they would ask all kinds of questions like her mother was asking now. There was no way Maggie could dodge them for long or lie to the people closest to her. She just didn't want them to worry about her upcoming tests.

She knew she was strong enough to handle this. She'd called Eileen, her closest friend, who'd seen her through many dark days and shared some of the good times too. She'd arranged to meet Eileen after her initial appointment with Dr. Wooding tomorrow. If Dr. Wooding did a needle biopsy and Maggie didn't feel up to going home, she would stay with Eileen.

Maggie had asked for some time off from work. That hadn't been a problem, but Joan was. Maggie was grateful that she hadn't asked any probing questions, but the look on her face said much. Maggie knew that Joan was disappointed that Maggie didn't trust her enough to confide in her. Later, she promised. She'd explain to Joan later.

As far as the situation with Phil was concerned, it was over, so there was no point in discussing that. She was not about to reopen that hurt, especially with Joan or anyone else for that matter.

Maggie set her cup down, but before she could speak, her mother interrupted sharply. "Don't bother to say 'nothing', because I know different. I want you to know that whatever it is; I'm here for you, Maggie – your father and I both. Just like you were there for me when I had my troubles."

Tears welled up in Maggie's eyes. Before the teapot was drained Lenore knew about the lump in Maggie's left breast, tomorrow's appointment and the possibility of a lumpectomy, depending on the results of tomorrow's tests.

After a bit more prodding on Lenore's part, she also heard about the situation with Phil and his betrayal. Maggie admitted everything except his overnight stay. She didn't think she needed to share all the details with her mother. She was a big girl, and furthermore, some things were too personal and none of her mother's business.

Maggie was amazed at how much better she felt just talking about it. Her mother shared how scared she'd been when she'd found her lump.

"The worst part is the waiting, the not knowing and imagining the worst," Lenore admitted softly. She was having trouble believing that a young woman like Maggie, her own daughter, might have to undergo the same humiliating invasion of privacy she had.

"I'll come with you tomorrow," her mother offered.

"It's okay. I'll be all right. They're only doing the needle biopsy so I think I'll be home tomorrow night," Maggie assured her. Eileen would meet her after the procedure.

"Okay, if that's the way you want it, but you will let me know as soon as you know anything, right? And I will be going with you, if anything else is required. There will be no further discussion on that subject," she stated flatly.

Maggie knew better than to argue. She'd never won an argument with her mother yet, and she doubted that today would be the first one. She knew that she needed to save her energy for her real battle.

On the subject of Phil, Maggie said very little, other than she cared for him but it had been a mistake on her part. He had someone else. Lenore suggested that sometimes we draw the wrong conclusions, unless issues are discussed frankly. If she really cared for Phil, maybe she owed it to him and herself to give him a call and find out for sure.

Maggie said she'd think about it. Lenore knew that meant she wouldn't call him. By the time Lenore left, they had cried together, hugged, laughed and both felt immeasurably better for it.

Lenore was still in a state of shock about Maggie's lump. She knew that with each case of breast cancer in a family, the odds were higher for each remaining female member. That's why she had badgered Maggie about going for regular check-ups. And now her worst fear had become reality. Maggie might have breast cancer, too.

But this situation with Phil troubled Lenore, and she wondered if there was anything she could do about it. Was she willing to risk experiencing Maggie's wrath again by what Maggie might consider interfering?

CHAPTER TWENTY-FOUR

Maggie checked in at the admission desk of St. Joseph's Hospital at ten o'clock for what she hoped would turn out to be a lumpectomy only.

The three-hour drive into Saskatoon had been a long one. Lenore accompanied Maggie. The trip was punctuated with long stretches of silence, each in their own private hell but pretending they weren't, so that the other wouldn't notice or worry.

Lenore found it hard to believe how all the terrors of her own experience could come flooding back. She was so sure she'd put that all behind her in her determination to be well again. It had only taken Maggie's crisis to trigger all her fears, this time for her only daughter rather than herself. Despite this, she was grateful Maggie had finally told her about it. It gave Lenore an opportunity to be there for her. Lenore knew firsthand how important it was to have the positive support and encouragement of those you love.

Maggie wondered if she would end up like her mother, half-breasted. She had more questions than answers these days. Every time she thought of something else, her mind would take hold of the idea and run with it. Minutes and sometimes hours later, she would find she'd been way out on a tangent of terror miles away from the original thought. It was good to have her mother with her, if for no other reason than that she brought Maggie back to the present and away from the horrors of 'what if.'

The call had come yesterday. The results from the needle biopsy were inconclusive. Fortunately for Maggie, a patient of Dr. Wooding's who was scheduled for a similar procedure today had suffered a heart attack Tuesday, allowing them to fit Maggie into that time slot. Her waiting would soon be over, and she'd know what she was dealing with.

Instead of allowing her imagination the freedom to wander again down the path of panic, Maggie thought about the visit she'd had with her friend Eileen just two days before.

Eileen, bless her heart, knew Maggie was putting on a brave façade. Because Eileen was one to confront issues, not skirt around them, she confronted Maggie. Maggie caved in. Soon she knew about Maggie's pigheadedness, her unwillingness to discuss her health problems or the situation with Phil.

Eileen had said she was being selfish and foolish where Phil was concerned. In fact, Eileen recommended that she have a psychiatrist check her head after the business with her breast lump was resolved. A woman with half a brain would not throw away a chance like the one Maggie had with Phil, unless she was crazy or stupid. To not even hear the guy's explanation about this perceived betrayal was absurd.

"Just how many chances do you think come along in one lifetime, Maggie?" Eileen had asked, totally flabbergasted. "He sounds like the one with whom you can make the life you always dreamed of happen. Don't be so quick to throw it all away."

All Maggie arguments were swept away by Eileen's ability to face reality. Even Maggie began to consider that perhaps she had reacted too hastily – just maybe.

Eileen lent Maggie a couple books. "Read them," she instructed firmly. "They sure helped me see things from a different perspective. Maybe they can help you, too."

Maggie read far into the night after she got home. She was sore from the biopsy and couldn't sleep, so she read and lay in the dark contemplating her situation. Maggie began to recognize that she'd been shutting herself off from life in an attempt to avoid pain. It clearly wasn't working. Maybe Eileen had a point, that to really live it's necessary to open oneself up to life and all its possibilities. Could she take that risk?

Perhaps when this was behind her, she'd have to reconsider the situation with Phil, providing there still was a situation with Phil. The possibility that he was involved with someone else haunted her.

Maggie was directed to take her forms and proceed to day surgery. On the surface, she appeared to be a confident, controlled woman, however, her insides were trembling, her mouth was dry as parchment, and her head was slightly dizzy. Her legs moved sluggishly, like blocks of wood grating against each other.

During the phone conversation with Dr. Wooding yesterday, they had elected to do a lumpectomy, which involved removing the tumor plus a cuff of healthy tissue surrounding it. They would also remove lymph nodes from her armpit to be certain there was nothing amiss there. They prepared her for the worst case scenario – that she could lose her breast if the lump turned out to be cancerous.

Maggie reminded herself that this would all be over in a few hours, and she would know what her future held.

The waiting area was as pleasant as it was possible to make it. The raspberry-colored chairs were placed in cozy, intimate arrangements. An entire wall of glass overlooked the lawns and flowerbeds below. Directly opposite, a high counter ran the length of the waiting area. Behind it, nurses, clerks and receptionists shuffled papers and scurried noiselessly in and out of cubicles. At one end behind the desk were curtained windows. The door was situated around the corner. Periodically, a masked nurse in green garb would appear, drop off papers, speak quietly to one behind the desk and leave again.

The magazine selection held no appeal for Maggie. She sat and watched and waited anxiously. Finally, a nurse about Maggie's size appeared, chart in hand. She told Lenore to stay where she was until Maggie was settled. She led Maggie into a room with two beds. A striped yellow and orange curtain had been pulled around the first bed.

The nurse introduced herself as Nancy and instructed Maggie to change into the clothes on the bed, being sure to have the opening to the front and wait there until someone came to get her.

Maggie's procedure was scheduled for eleven-thirty. Nancy told her they were running a bit late. She suggested Maggie change, then try to relax. At the absurdity of her suggestion to relax, Maggie chuckled. Nancy stopped short, thought for a minute about what she'd said, and a smile stretched across her face. It caused creases to form under her big blue eyes and around the corners of her mouth. The smile softened her entire face. Maggie liked her immediately.

"I say that all the time and don't realize how that must sound to you, under the circumstances. Silly, isn't it?" Nancy left, pulling the curtain shut behind her.

Maggie discovered to her amazement that the thin blue cotton pajamas assigned her were sufficiently large. In fact, if the bottoms hadn't had a tie string waist they would have dropped down around her ankles when she stood up. The top was too big as well. It had one tie at the neck, so she overlapped the tails and tucked them into the drawers. She was slipping into the white terry cloth slippers when she heard a commotion in the hall outside her room.

"I'm sorry, sir. You can't go in there." It sounded like Nancy, her voice loud and authoritarian, in sharp contrast to the hushed and muted sounds regularly heard here. "Sir, you must wait in the waiting…"

At that moment, the curtain snapped open, and there stood Phil. For an instant he stared at Maggie, then he turned to a distraught Nancy and ordered firmly, "You will excuse us, nurse," he said. "I need to speak to Maggie. I'll only be a few minutes. Then I will wait in the proper place."

With that, he stepped forward and ripped the curtain closed in Nancy's dazed face. Then Phil turned to face Maggie.

Maggie was as astonished as the nurse. "Phil, what…"

He crossed the distance between them in two steps, yanked her off the chair and into his arms. His mouth clamped down on hers and savagely possessed it. It was more a move to stake his claim than an expression of endearment. That could wait till later, he reasoned.

As abruptly as he pulled her from the chair, he now pushed her into it. A good thing too, because Maggie was so weak she feared she might faint. He squatted in front of her, so their eyes were nearly level, tightly clasping her hands between his much larger ones.

"Maggie, just listen for one minute. I know you said you didn't want to see me anymore, but there are a few things I need to say to you."

He was flushed and still slightly out of breath. His right eye was twitching wildly. A trickle of perspiration crept along the curve of his cheek in front of his ear and down his neck. The collar of his shirt was slightly askew on one side, as though he'd ripped his tie off

149

in haste. The trickle reached the collar, seeped into the fabric.

Maggie saw the undiluted fear in his eyes, which caused them to turn several shades darker than his normal coffee brown.

He was squeezing her hands so tightly that they were beginning to numb. Before she could utter a word, he continued. "I love you, Maggie. I have no idea what went wrong, but I want you to know that we are going to talk this through, face to face. Just as soon as you are able."

Maggie was dumbstruck. She couldn't understand why he was there. How did he know where to find her? Did he know why she was there?

As though reading her thoughts, he rushed on. "I've been pestering Jon to find out what was happening with you. So I know why you are here." He leaned closer and said quietly, "And Maggie Love, I need you to know that it doesn't matter to me if you have one breast or two or none. It doesn't matter if we can never have a family. What matters is that I love you and that you will be okay. And you led me to believe that you loved me too."

He brought her numbed hands to his mouth and kissed them tenderly, never taking his eyes off hers. "Please, Maggie, let me help you through this. Don't push me away again," he pleaded. "Whatever the problem is, we can work it out."

Maggie drew her hand from his and laid it along his cheek. It was smooth and warm. How she had missed touching him and being touched! The love she felt for him, that she'd tried to bury, gushed through her body, warming her insides till she thought she would glow.

Then she remembered how happy and carefree he'd appeared the day she saw him with that woman in the mall. She also remembered the searing pain that cut through her insides at his betrayal. But if he had a relationship with that thin, pretty woman, why was he here now? Why was he telling her he loved her? This was all so confusing.

"Sir! You must leave now!" Standing behind Phil with her fists punctuating her ample hips was a stern-looking Nancy. Neither Maggie nor Phil had noticed her. They looked at her and then at each other and smiled simultaneously. Even Nancy softened a little but did not move.

Phil rose, leaned over and gently loosened the tie on Maggie's hospital gown. Lightly he planted a kiss on each breast and then one on her trembling lips. He whispered, "They are beautiful, Maggie, but we can live without them." He retied the gown. "I'd better go before I get thrown out," he said aloud, as he cast a sideways glance at Nancy. The grin deepened his adorable dimples. His twitching ceased.

"We'd better talk later," Maggie managed.

"I'll be waiting for you, Maggie Love." With that, Phil stepped back and his smiling face disappeared behind the striped curtain.

Relief flooded Maggie's body as she sank back into the chair. In that instant, she knew that whatever happened, she would be okay. Phil must really love her if he still wanted her, with or without breasts, children or no children. Even though she'd been trying to convince herself that she could be happy without him, she loved him with all her heart. But what about that other woman? She'd have to find out. Maybe her mother was right again. Maybe there was a reasonable explanation.

Nancy moved the curtain aside to check that Phil had really left and wasn't lurking in the hallway. Then she turned back to Maggie and, with a grin a mile wide, declared, "What a hunk! If you don't want him, Maggie, you can toss him in my direction while you get your head examined."

Maggie wondered if maybe she did need to see a psychiatrist. Maybe all that was necessary was to open herself up to what life had to offer and not fight it. This wasn't what she had planned. Her life had taken detours and paths she hadn't considered or even wanted. It all seemed to be happening, whether she was ready or not. But maybe the magic that would make her life joyous and worthwhile was within her grasp if she would go with the flow and give Phil a chance. What a thought! But... later.

Maggie was still perplexed by Phil's actions. Shouldn't he be in school? Was any of this real? There was no time for the shock to wear off or for understanding to penetrate her brain. Minutes later the operating room nurse came to get Maggie.

CHAPTER TWENTY-FIVE

Phil was going crazy. They had been sitting in the waiting room for over an hour now, and still no word. He paced till he received a warning glare from one of the nurses. He flipped through several sports magazines but couldn't concentrate, so he threw them back on the pile. He watched Lenore out of the corner of his eye. She sat quietly; her hands folded loosely in her lap. She looked like she was somewhere else, meditating perhaps.

Phil's agitation broke through Lenore's calm. She became aware that he was watching her. She gestured for him to sit down, then suggested, "Maybe we should go find some coffee. By the time we get back, I'm sure she'll be finished. Okay?"

Reluctantly he agreed, even though he didn't want to be gone when she came back from surgery. Lenore took his arm, and they walked to the cafeteria, leaving a grateful staff behind.

"How do you stay so calm, Mrs. Mills?" Phil asked as they strode through the echoing corridors.

"I was praying. It helps me relax and stay focused. I've had some practice these past couple years," she said, more calmly than she felt. She worked very hard at not letting her emotions run uncontrolled.

Phil bought the coffee while Lenore found a table near a window. Just outside the window, a grounds-keeper was trimming the grass along the sidewalks with impeccable precision. They watched in silence.

Lenore saw this as her opportunity to get to know this man who'd captured her daughter's heart. Maybe he'd be more forthright than Maggie was, and she'd discover the reason for the rift in their relationship. Maggie had been pretty evasive about the details, even though she had shared with her mother that she cared deeply about this man. She'd only said that it was over. Maggie believed there was another woman.

152

Lenore watched him shift his attention from the gardener to his steaming coffee, take a scalding gulp and stare some more. He was obviously upset and anxious. Watching him made Lenore aware of the kind of hell her family had gone through when it was her in surgery, but none of them let on how worried they'd been.

"Phil, we don't know each other very well, but I believe one thing is true. We both care about Maggie. Now, as you probably already know, Maggie keeps a lot to herself."

Phil snorted at that, nodding his head. "She doesn't trust easily, I know."

Without mincing words, Lenore asked point blank, "Then tell me what happened between you two."

Phil raised his startled gaze to Lenore's. He took another gulp of coffee before answering. "I've been trying to figure that out for weeks now. I haven't got a clue. If you know, I'd sure appreciate your filling me in here."

Lenore felt compassion for this big brawny man, who was so obviously in love with Maggie, but bewildered by her rejection.

Lenore told him what little she knew. She recounted her conversation with Maggie the evening Lenore confronted her. When she added that Maggie believed Phil was seeing someone else, he nearly leaped from his seat. Then he settled back down and leaned back, totally deflated. He asked in disbelief, "She thinks what? How can she think that? That's absolutely ridiculous. Ridiculous!" He punctuated the statement by pounding his fist on the table and drawing the stares of other patrons.

"I'm sorry, Phil. That's all I could get out of her. She's been hurt, you know."

"I'm aware of that. But I'm not Richard. Why can't she see that?" he asked desperately.

When Maggie opened one eye, she was conscious of two things. Her hand hurt, and she was very thirsty. She glanced down at her left hand. It rested on top of the white cotton blanket with a Band-Aid across the back of it. Her right was held in the vice grip of Phil's, her fingers mashed together from the force. As soon as she moved, his eyes flew to her face and he rose to stand over her.

"It's okay, Maggie. You're going to be just fine."

She could see he was not the same intensely worried man she'd seen earlier snapping at Nancy. Her mother was beside him at her bedside instantly, rubbing her leg. Maggie hoped that the tears she saw in her eyes were tears of joy.

"Water," she croaked.

Lenore poured the water and handed it to Phil. She reached for a tissue to dab her eyes while Phil held the glass for Maggie to take a sip through the straw.

Maggie drank gratefully, then wet her lips with the moisture. Even this little effort left her weary. Closing her eyes again, she whispered, "The lump, what..."

"Everything is okay, Maggie. They found nothing that looked suspicious. Dr. Wooding said the tissue around the lump appeared normal. Nothing to worry about," Lenore explained, making no attempt to hide the tears now.

"Oh..." was all Maggie could say before she fell asleep again.

Maggie slept for another hour. This time she was more alert when she awoke. She wondered whether she'd dreamt it or if it was fact, that the lump was gone and everything was okay. She lifted her bandaged hand to her left breast. It too was bandaged, but, most important, it was still there! She looked around. The striped curtain was pulled around her bed, and her mother and Phil were sitting and talking in hushed tones beside her.

The curtain rattled open. Nancy appeared with a tray. "Have a good nap, Maggie?" she inquired, plunking the tray on the bedside table. "Looks like you're outta here as soon as you eat and pee. Are you ready to sit up?"

"Sure," was Maggie's uncertain reply.

Ready or not, Nancy was cranking the bed into a sitting position. Casting a stinging look at Phil, she added, "If you would like, Maggie, I will show this gentleman to the waiting room."

Straightening the sheet across her lap, Maggie answered, "No, it's okay. Thank you."

"Buzz if you need anything, Okay?" With that, Nancy breezed out of the room.

"Wow, what a charmer," Phil remarked, his eyes following her from the room.

"I'm sure she means well," Lenore defended.

An hour and a half later, Maggie was ready to leave, having drank the tea, eaten the pudding without nausea, and made the obligatory trip to the bathroom. Phil waited while Lenore helped Maggie get dressed.

Nancy told her the lab results – the official word about the surgery would take about a week, but the lump did not appear to be malignant. She explained how to care for her incisions and to report to Dr. Staeger about having the stitches removed. She also gave her several sheets of written instructions and a couple of painkillers for the trip home.

Lenore drove Maggie's car, with Maggie propped up and cushioned with pillows in the back seat. Phil followed in his.

The drive back home seemed longer than its normal three hours. Maggie dozed intermittently. After an hour or so, they stopped to pick up sandwiches and coffee. Neither Lenore nor Phil had eaten much all day.

Maggie, opening her eyes, joked lamely, "This is probably the only time you'll hear me say that I don't feel like eating," when Phil checked to see if she wanted anything.

Phil leaned into the car and kissed Maggie gently. "Just as soon as you feel up to it, I'll take you out for a big juicy steak or whatever suits your fancy. We'll celebrate in style," he said.

"Promises, promises," she said weakly.

"I am a man of my word. I thought you knew that about me, Maggie Love. Seems we have a few issues to address."

CHAPTER TWENTY-SIX

Maggie spent the first night at her parents' home, with Lenore and Jackson fussing over her. Maggie had little energy to argue, even though she thought she would sleep better in her own bed.

After Maggie was settled, Phil dropped in at Wayne and Joan's place, looking for a bed. They didn't inquire about his unexpected appearance, and he didn't offer an explanation. He could explain tomorrow. He was totally exhausted. Only when he laid his head on the pillow did he realize how draining the emotional roller coaster was that he'd been on for weeks now. His prayer of gratitude was heartfelt and short, as sleep overtook him within minutes.

Phil stopped by Maggie's parents' house just after noon the following day. He interrupted an argument that was raging. Maggie was insisting on going home against her parents' wishes. Lenore and Jackson finally relented with the understanding that Maggie would call if she needed anything. Phil offered to take her.

Once safely out of the driveway, Maggie relaxed. "I'm okay. Why do they need to hover like that?" she asked, exasperated.

Phil had never seen this side of Maggie. In that instant, he knew she would behave exactly the same with her own child as her mother had just demonstrated, and he loved her for it. "They worry about you. I think the relief is so great for your mom that she's almost beside herself," Phil defended.

During the previous day at the hospital, he'd gotten to know Maggie's mother a little. She was a smart, intuitive lady. He came to realize that Maggie had inherited her directness and strength from her mother. He respected them both. He had a feeling that he was going to get along with Lenore just fine.

"I know they mean well, but today their concern is stifling. Then I feel guilty about being short with them." She leaned her head back against the headrest, closed her eyes, and allowed a mountainous sigh to escape.

Phil studied her. She was pale and her hair slightly messed. He didn't know what to attribute her paleness to – pain, weakness, emotion or no make-up. He realized that even though she was a totally competent woman, this was a time when she needed nurturing. But she hated every second of being at someone else's mercy. She loathed the lack of independence that represented. Her vulnerability was showing, and it made him love her more. He took it as a sign of trust.

He reached over and took her hand, giving it a squeeze. "It's okay! We'll all feel better in a few days."

Phil unlocked the door and carried her things in when they reached her apartment. Maggie excused herself and went into the bathroom.

Gazing into the mirror at her image in this unflattering sweat suit, Maggie felt fat and unattractive. She knew they'd removed some flesh, not added any. That wasn't reassuring at the moment, but for now, comfort had to be her first concern, so the sweat suit stayed. At least it was a good color for her, royal blue. A few minutes later, she reappeared refreshed, having scrubbed her face and brushed her hair.

"That feels better." And it did feel somewhat better. Watching him hang her jacket in the closet, she said, "Thanks for bringing my stuff in. Would you like some coffee?"

"Shouldn't you have a rest or something?" He was surprised by her offer.

"I'm fine, but I'll be better when I've had some coffee," she said heading for the kitchen. "Mom wouldn't let me have any this morning. She said it made her sick after she'd had anesthetic, so I shouldn't have any either. Did you ever hear anything so silly?"

Phil came up behind her at the counter as she reached for the coffeepot and took it out of her hand. His other hand rested lightly on her shoulder. "How about letting me make coffee, Maggie?" he asked quietly.

She glanced over her shoulder into those warm brown eyes. For all his massiveness, he appeared ready to crumble like an old Scottish stone wall if she refused. He too was vulnerable, she realized. She surrendered the coffeepot without protest.

"Then we'll talk," she said, putting two cheery yellow striped placemats on the table.

"Only if you're certain you feel up to this, Maggie. It can wait till another day when you're feeling stronger." Even though he desperately needed to hear Maggie's explanation before he could make any sense out of the past few weeks, he could stand the bewilderment a while longer until Maggie had her strength back. That was his first concern right now.

"No. Let's get a few things straightened out," she answered quietly but firmly.

She eased herself slowly into a chair. There was no pain unless she moved her left arm or bumped into something. She'd been assured that would be temporary, until the incisions healed. Once she was settled, she sat still.

She'd spent much of last night, between the painkiller-induced naps, wondering what was going on with Phil, now that her cancer scare was behind her and no longer her primary concern. She knew it was time to clear the air.

Phil took a seat.

Maggie thought he looked more fragile and apprehensive than she felt. The dark smudges under his eyes indicated that he hadn't slept well either. She wondered how long it had been since he'd had a restful night's sleep. She couldn't let sympathy get in the way.

Phil knew there was no point in small talk. Whether she was in pain or not was irrelevant. Maggie's determination showed in the set of her jaw.

They studied each other in silence as the coffeepot gurgled away. She could see the confusion in his eyes, he the pain in hers.

As he set her steaming mug of coffee in front of her and slid into his chair again, he said, "Maggie, I have no idea what went wrong between us. I'm totally baffled. I've been trying to figure it out for weeks, and I'm no wiser now. If I've hurt you in some way, I'm sorry. That was never my intention. I love you. But you need to trust me enough to tell me what the problem is."

Maggie was feeling very fragile. He'd just hit the nail on the head – trust. She'd been so afraid to trust him with her heart. She stared at her hands, wrapped tightly around the yellow mug. The memory of the heart-wrenching pain she'd been through was fresh and clear, just under the surface of her control.

She knew if she looked into his brown eyes, she might not be able to talk, so she stared at her hands, took a deep breath and began. "I went to Prince Albert for a mammogram in early June, the week after our camping trip. After the test was over, I went to the mall for coffee before calling you. I wanted to compose myself. The mammogram clearly showed a lump, but what it was, nobody knew yet. A biopsy was the next step." She glanced quickly at Phil's face to see that he was following her story, then back to her hands. She continued, "I saw you in the jewelry store across from where I was sitting, with a woman. You appeared to know each other very well. You were laughing and seemed to be having a good time, checking out what looked like rings." She paused, again checked Phil's reaction.

His brow was creased in thought, trying to recall the day Maggie was talking about.

Watching him closely, she added, "When you touched her as you went through the doors, it looked to me as though you were intimately involved with this cute little woman. It appeared more than casual. So I decided to end it before I got more entangled or committed, and hurt again. I didn't think I could cope with that pain again. Besides, I had this lump to deal with."

Phil stared at her in disbelief. For the life of him, he couldn't remember the day in question. "Maggie, I have no idea what day or who you could have..." He stopped abruptly, remembering. The puzzled look vanished. "Booth's Jewelers? In the downtown mall?"

Maggie nodded.

"I know now. That was Jeanette Campbell. She's a teacher on staff. We had the chore of picking out a retirement gift for one of our old-timers, George Kane. He's been the head custodian at the school for more years than any of us can remember. We were pretty excited because George had said once that he always wanted a pocket watch like he remembered his grandfather wearing. We found one in Booth's. While we were waiting to have it engraved, I told Jeanette about us. She warned me that I'd better not let you slip away. Then she pointed out a few rings she thought you might like." He stopped, worry lines creasing his forehead. "I was looking for a ring for you, Maggie."

He reached for her hands, pried her fingers loose from the coffee mug, and pressed them between his own. "Jeanette is a great gal, a good teacher, and I enjoy her enthusiasm. Besides, she's married to an insurance agent and has three small kids. Nice family. There is nothing but respect between us, nothing more."

Maggie was ashamed. She had jumped to conclusions, just as her mother suggested. The tears were beginning to pool at the corners of her eyes, so she kept them lowered.

"I didn't know you were coming into Prince Albert. Why didn't you tell me? Did you know about this appointment that weekend we spent together at Little Bear Lake?"

She nodded without looking up.

It was obvious she didn't trust him enough to tell him what was happening in her life. He could feel his anger building. All this anguish because she was having trouble trusting him. He wasn't Richard! How could he make her understand that?

Tears were rolling down her cheeks. She pulled her hands from his and reached for a tissue on the counter. She wiped her eyes. Looking at him she saw his jaw tighten, his eyes darken in fury.

"Yes, I knew about the lump that weekend, but I didn't want to spoil the magic of our time together. I rationalized my actions. I told myself that we really had made no kind of a commitment to each other. Besides that, I felt I needed to know I could get through this on my own. And when I thought I might be ready to share that with you, I saw you with that woman. I believed you had changed your mind about us... that you would rather have someone else." She caught her breath and whispered, "Someone prettier or not so big."

Phil's anger exploded. His eye began twitching uncontrollably. He flew out of his chair to pace back and forth. He stopped, braced his fists on the back of the chair he'd just vacated and facing Maggie yelled, "Big! Big! What are you talking about? Your body is perfect as far as I'm concerned. It's you who seems to have a problem with your size, not me, Maggie." He stopped and raked his hands through his hair. His frustration overflowed. "I thought you knew me better than that. I thought I'd made that quite plain to you. It seems you also have a problem with trust. From my point of view, we took this getting to know each other business pretty slow. I understood the need for that. That jerk Richard hurt you deeply. I know that. But dammit, I'm not Richard! How do I convince you of that? I won't ever intentionally hurt you, Maggie."

Maggie watched him and knew that he was right. What he said rang true. It was she who'd hurt him with her suspicions. Just like Eileen had warned her, she couldn't close herself off, thinking that action would prevent any further sorrow in her life. In that instant, a light clicked on. This was her life, whether she was ready for it or not, joys and sorrows. She'd better get on with really living, rather than trying to avoid circumstances that could be painful or unpleasant. So far, she'd allowed her fears to paralyze her.

"I'm sorry, Phil. I never stopped to think how my behavior would affect you. I was so afraid. I was so wrapped up in getting through all this without losing my mind that I overlooked your feelings. I can see now how selfish that was of me. But I was certain that if I lost my breast, I would be revolted by my own body, so how could you possibly accept it?" She looked at him questioningly.

He stood facing her, his knuckles white from gripping the back of the chair. "Like I told you at the hospital, one breast, two or none, doesn't matter. I love you, Maggie, the person you are. The body is just the package. That changes over the years, at least mine has, but that doesn't change how I feel." He searched her face for understanding, watching the tears stream down her cheeks. "I'm really sorry that I didn't make that crystal clear before now."

Maggie had never felt so humbled in her life. She had assumed thoughts and feelings for Phil that he'd never had. He had opened up his life to her and was offering his love. All she had to do was trust him. She knew it was time to try. She reached out to him with her right hand. He took it and held it gently as though it was her heart.

"I'm going to try very hard. Please, be patient with me, Phil. Letting my guard down, letting you get close to me, really close, is scary."

"I'll tell you as often as you need to hear it, Maggie. I love you. I love every inch of you, body, mind and soul."

He yanked his chair out, sat down, and pulled it up to hers. With their knees touching, he gently wiped her tears with his thumbs, smoothing them away as one might with a hurt child.

Maggie leaned forward till their foreheads met. A pain shot through her from the movement, making her grimace.

"What's the matter? Does it hurt?" Phil stilled her with his hand on her shoulder.

"No, it's okay. It just pulled for a second. That's all."

She was tired, like all the starch had been drained out of her, like a wave had rolled over her, leaving her exhausted. But she needed to continue. "I love you too, Phil. I have for some time, but I was so afraid to give in to it completely, so afraid to take the risk. I see that now. I'm sorry for the pain I've caused us both."

He held her face in his hands again and kissed her reddened eyes, her tear-stained cheeks, her raw nose, and finally her lips. He tasted the salty tears that had dried there. Pulling back, he peered deep into her blue, blue eyes and proclaimed, "We will make a life together, Maggie, you and I."

Maggie smiled weakly and nodded.

Phil could see the exhaustion, the paleness. "Now that we have that settled, you are going to have a rest. Everything else will wait till you are feeling stronger."

There were so many things she still didn't understand. She'd have to ask him later. Her heart had just opened, and now she was anxious to share it with Phil, to talk, laugh, touch and be touched. Her heart leapt at the notion, but her body did not.

Maggie was impatient with her body's need to rest, but she knew it was necessary for her recovery, both physical and emotional. She agreed to rest when he assured her he would stay while she slept. Her own bed felt wonderfully comforting.

He tucked the quilt up under her chin and lovingly ordered her to sleep, tenderly kissed her, and closed the door.

Several hours later, she awoke to a mouth-watering aroma coming from her kitchen. Slowly she eased herself off the bed and found her slippers.

She couldn't decide what was cooking. It smelled like chicken.

When she rounded the corner into the kitchen, she stopped short. She leaned against the door jam and drank in the sight.

Phil was wearing a dishtowel tucked into his jeans, his hands in dough, flour to his elbows. It looked like he was making biscuits. One of her cookbooks was propped up on the windowsill, a pot simmered on the stove. He turned when he heard her chuckle.

"Hi," he greeted her. "I hope I didn't wake you. How are you feeling?" He dusted his hands off over the sink and washed them before he crossed to where she was leaning against the doorway and kissed her lightly.

"I'm much better. What are you making? It smells wonderful. I didn't know you could cook."

Cocking his head to one side, he studied her. "There are plenty of things you don't know about me, my love. You're in for quite a treat." Running his hands over his midsection, he added, "How do you suppose I got to look like this? I know my way around a kitchen."

She held her side as she laughed softly, so it wouldn't cause any pain.

While he finished supper, Maggie had a bath. At least as much as was possible with her bandages. Carefully, she washed her hair with her right hand. It was awkward and took much longer than usual, but she managed. When she was toweled dry and dressed in a lounger, she felt refreshed and ravenously hungry.

While she was sleeping, Phil had slipped out to the store to get a few groceries and a bunch of flowers. His mother had maintained that chicken soup was the remedy for any ailment. It had always worked in his family, so maybe Maggie would appreciate a bowl too. Both his previous wives, Sandra and Shelley, passionately believed that any situation, good or bad, could be improved with flowers. Mentally he thanked them for that advice as he chose daisies for Maggie. They winked cheerfully at them from the centre of the table.

Maggie looked more rested. A rosy color had returned to her cheeks.

When she appeared at the table he'd set with special care, he had the urge to hug her tightly to him. Knowing that wasn't possible, he held her gently, careful not to put any pressure on her breast. While she rested her head against his shoulder, he cautiously rubbed her back.

"You look wonderful. Smell good too. Hungry?"

"Starved."

"Have a seat," he said, pulling out a chair for her. "Supper is served."

The soup was scrumptious, the biscuits hot and fluffy. While they ate, she asked him the questions that had plagued her.

He explained about running into Jon at the driving range, their conversation, how Phil had badgered him into finding out what was happening. He told her that Jon had called Lenore. When Lenore finally extracted the truth from Maggie, the telephone relay worked its way back to Phil. Jon did his best to fill him in on the whole business with the lump and surgery.

Phil had taken his report cards to school that last day and asked his principal to hand them out. He told him that an emergency had arisen and he needed to leave immediately. He drove like a maniac to Saskatoon to be there in time for Maggie's surgery. He'd needed to see her before the surgery. It was imperative that she know how he felt before they knew the outcome of the surgery.

His spoon stopped in mid-air as he remembered that day. "I'm sorry that I was so abrupt, maybe even rude to that nurse, but I had to see you. Extraordinary circumstances called for extraordinary measures."

Maggie laughed. "You mean Nancy. She wasn't too hurt. In fact, she thinks you're a hunk. She told me that if I didn't hang onto you, I should have my head examined."

Phil shook his head, eyes wide. "She did?"

"Yup. I've decided she's right. You're my kinda guy. And one who makes delicious chicken soup besides." Maggie brushed an overlooked smear of flour from Phil's sleeve and left her hand resting on his arm.

"Thanks. Cooking is just one of my many talents. Now that school is out, I have nearly all summer to impress you." An impish grin deepened his dimples. Maggie's mind flashed back to a weekend that now seemed like ages ago. "I'd like that." She could feel the red blotches rising from beneath her collar. Her memories created a stirring in her middle.

He took her hand. The tingling started at her fingertips when he kissed them and traveled all the way to her heart. It sent hot blasts of blood burning through her veins. Was it possible that she could feel sexually aroused this soon after surgery? That thought was instantly erased by the pain that resulted from shifting in her chair. Such things would have to wait till she healed. Today, just knowing she was loved and cherished was enough. She would relax and relish these blissful moments that were like a soothing, healing balm for her body and spirit.

CHAPTER TWENTY-SEVEN

Between Phil and Lenore, they saw to it that Maggie was well cared for. No request fell on deaf ears. Maggie saw firsthand how adept Phil was in the kitchen, at wielding a vacuum cleaner, and scrubbing a toilet.

Phil and Lenore convinced Maggie, who normally had little patience with being ill, that rest was the best medicine. She had no idea that any man could be so attentive and caring. If ever she had doubted his love, she no longer could. He proved it in the countless loving gestures he made for her day after day. He brushed her hair, dusted her bell collection, sorted her CD's alphabetically, read poems aloud from her Robert Service collection, played her own and his favorite music and massaged her back and neck.

Phil slept at Wayne and Joan's place but spent his days with Maggie. Phil knew he must not stay the night. By the time he left, he ached. He'd never realized how much discipline and strength it took to restrain his instincts to ravish Maggie. He wanted her desperately, and being with her daily had him in a near constant state of arousal. Not only did he want to make love with her, but he needed her to know without a doubt that he would love, nurture, and protect her.

As the days passed, her incisions healed. The stitches were removed, and the much-anticipated report arrived with the lab results they had prayed for. There was no cancer. Her body reminded her often that the need for healing was foremost, before the need for sexual expression. Maggie sensed Phil's controlled sexual energy. Soon her own impatience spilled over.

She'd been leaning back in the armchair, listening to a recording of ocean sounds that Phil had brought to share with her, while he cleared away the supper dishes. She drifted off. Upon waking, she sensed his presence. Phil was perched on the footstool, calmly watching her sleep. His quiet, constant concern ignited a blaze in

Maggie. She lifted her right hand to reach for him. He took it and rubbed it tenderly. His gentleness made him so lovable.

"Do you know what I'd like to do right this minute?" she asked, wiggling to ease the warm sensations in her groin. The tempo of the pounding surf from the stereo echoed through her body

"What?"

Quietly, without betraying the sensual rhythm coursing through her, she replied, "I'd like to tear all your clothes off and have you right here on the floor. Now."

His mouth dropped open. She watched his Adam's apple bob down and up again as he swallowed "You would?"

She remained reclining in her chair but squeezed his hand. "Does that shock you?"

"Yes and no. Yes, because I thought it was too soon, and no because I know you are an incredibly sexual woman." After studying her for a moment, he continued, "I'm also relieved because I'm finding it very difficult to be with you day after day and not be able to hold you, afraid to touch you. I want so badly to hold you against me and make love to you. But I don't want my loving to ever cause you pain, only joy." He leaned closer. He was totally unaware that he had her hands firmly clamped between his, while emotion flooded his face.

"It's been weeks since the surgery. I'm almost completely healed," she soothed. "Besides, my entire right side was untouched. Trust me, I'll let you know if something hurts."

Gently pulling Maggie to her feet, he asked, not quite believing her, "Are you certain about this?"

She reached her right arm around to encircle him in a gentle embrace, laying her cheek against his chest. "Mm... hmm. But I think the floor would be too uncomfortable just now. Another time, perhaps."

"Whatever your pleasure might be," he whispered, his lips scorching her ear.

"Slow and easy."

And so they did. He urged her to relax, enjoy and instruct him from movement to movement. It hurt him to see the bold redness of the scars, but he tenderly brushed his lips over the edges and felt

Maggie melt at his acceptance of her mutilated body and the pleasure that it could still bring.

The intensity they both felt was released in the ebb and flow of their lovemaking. It peaked when he ravished her mouth, teasing and twisting. Maggie responded like a thirsty woman at the well, drinking deep and often. He caressed her thoughtfully, purposely, expertly, watching her leave the consciousness of her body behind and float with the waves of sensation. His pleasure intensified, knowing he could please her and prolong his own gratification. When the release did come, much later, it was stunning, stupefying, and mutually satisfying.

Stretched out on his side facing Maggie, Phil's breath became more even. Contentment softened the tiny crinkles around his eyes and smoothed the lines that had gathered on his brow.

She savored the closeness and the rightness of the moment. There had been no pain, only pleasure.

As the sun sank behind the pines across the river, the warmth of twilight washed Maggie's bedroom in a cozy golden glow. She turned her face toward Phil, checking to see if he'd fallen asleep. Instead, he was looking at her, his brown eyes overflowing with love and satisfaction.

"How are you feeling?" he whispered, his thumb stroking her cheek.

Words were choked in her throat, words she needed to share. She kissed him tenderly and said, "Your loving is like a warm fuzzy blanket that you wrap around me. Not just my body but my soul too. You bring me such joy, pleasure beyond anything I've ever experienced… contentment and challenge."

His psyche, all that he was, cracked wide. He would offer her everything he was and would be. He would take the risk. Would she? "I love you, Maggie. I want to spend the rest of my life loving you."

"What if there's another lump? More surgery? What if it's cancer next time? What if we can't have a family? What if…" The questions rose again.

He placed his fingertips on her lips, "Sh-sh, Maggie Love. Whatever comes next, we can face it together, you and me, if you are willing," he reminded her of his commitment.

Maggie knew in that instant she had a choice to make. Whether she took the risk or not, it would profoundly affect the rest of her life. She was at a turning point.

In that moment, the message on the magnet stuck to Eileen's fridge flashed into Maggie head. She wished she could remember it exactly. It said that avoiding risk was no safer than facing life's challenges head on, because life was either a grand adventure or nothing at all. She felt the last of the wall she'd built around herself crumble.

She smiled and placed her hand on his chest over his heart. "I just realized that you are the love I have been waiting for all my life, and you were right here in my home town all along. I love you, Phil Sanders."

"Do I take that as a yes? Will you marry me, Maggie Mills?" he asked tentatively.

"Yes, yes, yes!" she laughed, tears of joy flooding her face.

He kissed her. Her answer jerked free the knots that had been tied in his stomach. In a lighthearted tone, he asked, "Does that mean I can spend the nights here until we get married?"

"Yes. Just don't tell my mother," she joked.

"She already knows. That and more," he revealed sheepishly.

Maggie raised an eyebrow. "More?"

"She's hoping for a late summer wedding."

"Oh?"

Phil kissed her open mouth. "What do you think we talked about while we waited all those long hours you were in surgery? I have to confess that your mother and I have become tight. We have an understanding."

"Tell me more."

"If I can insure a wedding this summer, she'll overlook the fact that I stay here, I'm sure," he smiled broadly, his dimples deepened.

"What a deal! You and my mother. Who would have thought?" Then she remembered that it was her mother who had championed Phil's case from the beginning. It wasn't really too surprising that they had become allies.

She embraced Phil as tightly as was possible. She knew that she was standing at the brink of her boldest, most challenging adventure, like a skydiver standing at the cliff's edge, poised to jump with complete faith in her parachute. Except this time Maggie was not alone. She would hold tight to the man she loved. She would take the gamble and see what life had in store for her. She was ready!

THE END